Treading On Egg Shells

Carole Sampson

To a special friend, Shirley.
Trusting you won't tread
on any eggshells whilst
reading this!
  With much love,
    Carole x

ISBN: 978-1-326-21301-5

PublishNation, London
www.publishnation.co.uk

CHAPTER 1

Meet the Harpers

The chickens lived at the bottom of the garden. They were kept purely for practical reasons. The eggs they laid aided my mother in the kitchen where she produced copious egg- based dishes to satisfy hungry children. Her omelettes were reknowned in the neighbourhood; she seemed to be able to produce fluffy, appetising half moons which melted as soon as your tongue touched them. Her Victoria Sponge and Dundee Fruit Cake won prizes at the annual village show, whilst the lightly boiled egg was always cooked to perfection; neither too hard or too soft. It was perfect for the soldiers of white bread cut into uniform pieces ready for dipping into the enticing yellow yolk and spread with lashings of golden butter.

The poached egg was made by cracking it open and dropping it into boiling water where it cooked for two or three minutes. I loved the way the albumen fluffed round the exposed yolk, protecting it from the harsh bubbles. How I hated the egg poacher eventually bought to ensure the perfect formation of the egg to be placed on toast, made by a toaster, no longer toasted against the flames of the open fire or on the Aga. Why would anyone choose a manufactured poacher over natural boiling water? I would never say anything to Mum; she could easily be offended by implied criticism. Always essential to tread gently with her. She was too precious to upset.

We rarely had scrambled egg at home because ' the pan's SO hard to clean,' although Dad occasionally offered to scrape it so that we could enjoy the coagulated yolks on buttered toast. My mouth waters at the thought of the delicious feast! I always felt that Dad was entitled to an opinion on the egg front. He fed, watered and tended the hens as well as cleaning out their house. As a child I would don my wellies and trot down the garden behind the mountain of a man who was my father. Some days we were only obliged to feed, water and collect eggs from the hens, but on cleaning days we had to enter the hen house and change the bedding of straw and rearrange the perching posts in order ' to give them a different view of the world.' Such a wise man. Considerate of the needs of everyone, including his beloved hens. We named them. It was easy to know them as individuals. Each one had its own markings and each one responded to its own name when he spoke it gently. Sometimes he stroked and petted them and they knew he cared.

Eggs that could not be used immediately were placed in a large earthenware lidded pot which was kept under the sink in the kitchen. Into this pot had been poured a peculiar substance called isinglass, which preserved the eggs until needed. Fridges were almost unheard of in England at this time and other ways had to be found to keep food edible.

When the chickens had stopped laying, they were used for the Sunday meal. I can remember with horror being told of Bella's fate as we sat down to Sunday dinner and father began to carve the beautiful breast of my favourite chicken. I could hardly contain my tears or my desire to warn her sisters of the fate which lay in store for them. My father told me that it was essential to use the birds as a source of food. I presume that I had not realized until that point that we ate our hand-reared chickens when their laying days were over. He was more philosophical than I was. Grown-ups need to be pragmatic in order to endure what life throws at them. In retrospect, my parents had survived two world wars, experienced the hardships of rationing, economic depression and the three day week. They had learned how to provide their own meals of meat and vegetables through self-sufficiency. They worked together to provide food, clothing and shelter for their family.

George was their eldest child. When I came along, he was already at secondary school and discussing his future career with our father and grandfather. I always felt that he resented my presence. I was an intrusion, not necessary to his cosy existence. Elizabeth, on the other hand, being two years younger than George, welcomed this little doll into her home. She petted me and made me feel cherished beyond all expectations. As she had only been two (and a half, as she always corrected everyone who spoke about differences in ages) when Stuart was born, she had been too young to act as his second mother, so she was able to use up her maternal instincts with me. Lizzie and I were soul mates, but we allowed Stuart into our tiny circle unless he became too rough. The ten years between us were sufficient for it not to be a problem. She mothered me and I lapped it up! She and Stuart both had gentle, tolerant natures, loving each other and the world. Except....

George. He was belligerent. Always difficult to please. Always opinionated. Often resentful, especially of this adopted baby who had arrived in his home because of a war and a wayward woman. Why had his parents felt that they needed to give someone else's child a home? Hadn't they got a big enough family? Weren't he and his siblings meant to be the result of their special union? Why did they need an intruder? Why had they responded to their Vicar's pleas for people to come forward and offer a home to an unwanted baby? He knew that one had to be open hearted, but he had always accepted Elizabeth and Stuart. His parents had used Jesus' words, ' Suffer little children to come unto me and forbid them not,' as a weapon. He knew, in his heart of hearts, that this was right but his feelings for 'Little Judith' were ones of resentment and mistrust.

I knew instinctively that he did not care for me and as I got older, Elizabeth taught me how to circumvent trouble with him. I was to be careful in what I commented on, let him have his own way to avoid conflict and allow our parents to discipline him in order to bring him to reasonableness. What a drag! Stuart and our big sister seemed to have learned how to do this. It was far more difficult for me. I wondered if it was because I was not from the same genes, but Lizzie assured me that the fault lay with him.

There were often scraps between us which usually resulted in either Stuart or me running to mother's side in tears. Usually Lizzie supported we younger pair if the incident involved George, but she was capable of digging in her heels against Stuart.

I remember one awful incident which involved the four of us.

CHAPTER 2

Fox wars

Living in a village was idyllic. It was, as Peter Doggett commented in the sleeve notes of Ray Davies 'Village Green Preservation Society', " a fantasy place of refuge". We had fields backing onto the garden which stretched as far as the eye could see. Looking towards the horizon could sometimes be breathtaking as the sun shone bewitchingly through the branches of the trees, casting long shadows on the green land. By the end of August the farmer's field of yellowy beige fluttered in a gentle breeze. The oats had ripened and were ready for harvesting. Other corn fields stood erect, waiting for the thresher to come and sort the wheat from the chaff. Farmer Hobbs was possessive of his fields and we were not allowed to wander through them unless we kept to the designated pathways. Animals do not, however, understand the human farmers' rules. Field mice scamper amongst the corn stalks, rabbits hop along between the rows and Mr Fox hunts.

One night, the red-haired, handsome specimen made his way across the fields, through the tall, beech hedge at the bottom of our garden and followed the smell of chicken. How he managed to enter the chicken house we could not fathom. Father had used wire mesh, raised stakes and wooden slats to deter a hungry fox. Foxes can do so much damage; they don't always kill and eat, sometimes they just kill or maim. If they were hungry one could understand their behaviour, but when it is sport it is more difficult to forgive indiscriminate murder. No-one heard Mr Fox in the night; even the dogs did not bark. They were usually good alarm indicators, often being roused from their nap by the slightest sound, but on this particular night, nothing!

When father went out to feed his beloved hens the next morning he found devastation. Mr Fox had killed two hens. One was missing (obviously his evening meal) and the eggs were eaten or smashed, with broken egg shells littering the hen house. The hens that had escaped the massacre were sheltering inside their house, cowering from the world which had erupted like Vesuvius during the night. With a heavy heart Dad cleaned up as much as he could before coming back to the house for breakfast, where he related the sorry tale to his bleary - eyed family as they spooned their porridge into their mouths.

The Aga was a wonderful invention. Breakfast porridge was started on one of the two top rings and then transferred to the top right hand oven to complete its journey so that it would finish as a white, creamy, wholesome dish. Toast was put into a special flat grid with long handles and placed on top of the ring before the lid was closed onto it. After two minutes, it was turned and then given a final two minutes to complete browning. When it was spread with butter, no other accompaniment was needed for it to taste delicious.

I expect Mum fed me as I was only two years old at this time. She was probably ably assisted by Lizzie, whilst the boys would have scoffed their porridge in preparation for the delights of buttered toast.

Mum and Dad drank tea whilst we children all had a glass of milk. Camp coffee was not to my father's taste and only rarely appeared at a meal. When I was older and tasted it, I could understand why it was disliked. The coffee from today's Starbucks, Costa and Cafe Nero does not resemble liquid Camp coffee in any way. It is hard to believe they are the same animal!

Talking of which, the incident with Mr Fox had sown wicked thoughts in my eldest brother's mind, when the hens had been so unfairly mutilated. George had immediately suggested that the fox should be hunted down and dispatched. He wanted the chickens to live undisturbed. Our father said that he was only doing what his instincts commanded him.

"All creatures have a right to live," he smiled benignly.

A week after the debacle, George called a meeting in his bed room. Being a toddler, I don't think that I had been privy to such occasions before, but he had a plan which involved all of us. We three younger children were to go down to the hen house one evening, smash the eggs and then pretend to discover the mess. Stuart would then rush up to the house and fetch George who would in turn fetch our father. Lizzie could not see the point of the exercise but George explained that Dad would think it was Mr Fox and would therefore lay in wait for him, shoot him and we would never again be troubled.

"It is only what he deserves," explained George. "We need the eggs and chickens to be able to live decent lives and if he keeps doing this it will cause Mum and Dad lots of problems."

This clinched it and Lizzie capitulated which naturally meant that Stuart went along with the idea. I was too young to realize what we would be doing but Stuart assured me it would be fun.

The following evening we put the plan into action. George took us down to the hen house, unlocked it and put us inside. He encouraged me to stamp on the beautiful brown eggs and then retreated to the kitchen. We got out of the hen house and Stuart ran to fetch our older brother. He pretended to be outraged and ran into the house to summon our father.

" Quick! You should see what has happened!"

Dad must have rushed down the garden to survey the scene as though his life depended on it. He was obviously suspicious, especially as George began to shout,

"It was the fox, the fox!"

" I don't think so George. This is children's work," said our father looking round at all of us. His kind, blue eyes searched the faces of his off-spring and adopted daughter.

"It was Judith," said George. " She stamped on the eggs."

Lizzie began to protest. Stuart hung his head.

Father turned to us all.

" I think we should go back into the house," he urged, picking me up in his broad arms.

Once he had placed me in the play-pen he suggested that Lizzie help him clear up the mess in the hen house, whilst the boys busied themselves inside until supper time.

" Now, Lizzie. Let's hear your side of the story."

" We all thought that the fox should be hurt for causing so much damage. So, George had this idea. He made Judith stamp on the eggs. She's too little to know that she shouldn't do that."

" Why didn't you stop her?"

" It all went so quickly. George went back to the kitchen, and when we'd got out of the hen house, Stuart went up and fetched him as we'd arranged and I brought Judith out."

" Um....O.K.... We'll deal with it when we get back into the house. We'd best tidy up this mess first."

They worked companionably until the hen house was restored to order and the chickens could once more settle peaceably on their roosts.

When they got back into the kitchen, Dad gathered us together with our mother and told George he should be punished because at the age of fourteen, he was old enough to show responsibility. George flashed a menacing look in Lizzie's direction.

" If you'd seen Judith stamping on eggs, you should have stopped her and explained that she wasn't to do it."

" How could I stop her?" demanded George belligerently.

" You only have to lift her up in your arms and move her away. Anyway, how did she get in? She's too little to reach the latch, young man."

George knew that he had been rumbled. He hung his head in shame.

" I'm sorry, Dad," he mumbled.

" And so am I. I had hoped for something better from you. There's no pocket money for two weeks."

" Oh no."

" Oh yes. Now, let's all sit down and eat."

Mother had produced a lovely, rare scrambled egg on toast, which we ate with relish. All, except George. Pocket money was not a lot; one shilling for him and sixpence for Lizzie and Stuart. I was too young to be given my own money at this stage but I knew that it was very important to the others. It was independent means and as long as we were sensible with our purchases our parents allowed us to make choices. Lizzie always bought a 'School Friend' comic and a bar of chocolate. Stuart always spent his money on a toy and when I was older I usually bought a ' Girl' comic and a Kit-Kat or Mars bar. At this time George was saving his pocket money to buy accessories for his bike. He had almost saved enough for lights. Losing two weeks pocket money meant he would have to wait.

" The dark nights will be here and I shan't have any lights." He turned on me. " It's your fault," he shouted.

" Go to your room George, and calm down," suggested our mother. " You obviously don't want supper, and I'm not having you talk to Judith, or anyone, like that."

" Why we had to have her I don't know," spat George.

" Enough!" said our father in a stern voice, rising from his chair. "Go to your room. NOW!"

George knew he was beaten. He went out slamming the door behind him.

" Let him go, Mother. We'll deal with him later. Just let's eat."

There were going to be repercussions. I was not going to be able to forget that I was an interloper in George'e eyes. His jealousy and deep seated resentment could cloud a happy childhood unless I learned how to circumvent trouble from him.

I would have to learn from my sister and younger brother.

CHAPTER 3

Brotherly love

Brothers and sisters do not necessarily have the same natures, even if they come from the same gene pool. Our family was no exception.

Lizzie was gentle, kind, considerate and always seeking ways of helping others. Her disposition ensured that she had a happy countenance with a ready smile and sparkling eyes. Even when she was sad or 'under the weather,' she managed to maintain a dignity which I tried to emulate, despite not sharing her birth parents. Were my own birth mother and father also gentle and considerate, or did I learn these qualities from my big sister?

George was a handsome boy, tall for his age and resembled our father. There were delightful photographs of our parents in their courting days; an upright, young man over six feet tall alongside a demure, slight, fashionable, young woman. They were obviously in love and their kind, smiling faces signified their natures. Lizzie always said that she was sad that George had inherited our father's good looks but not his nature. He had a disagreeable disposition. He was quick to blow, like a steam engine leaving a station. His unpredictable changes of mood were alarming. One minute he could be charming, thoughtful and almost considerate, but this sense of harmony could be shattered into discord if somebody said the wrong thing and it did not have to be the same thing each time. George could react negatively or positively, depending on his mood. Mother always teased him with,

"Got out of the wrong side of bed this morning, did you?" whilst Dad told him to 'snap out of it.'

It was not as easy for us. Even Lizzie, with her good nature, was unable to jolly him along if he was ' on one.' On these occasions, she usually gave into his demands. Stuart was in awe of his big brother and as he got older had no difficulty in following George's lead and allowing him to take control.

As I think about it now, George had a tendency to bully when he was young.

Stuart was as small for his age as George was tall. He had the gentle, handsome features of our father and grandfather and their kind eyes, which made his peers listen to his opinions. By the time he was eleven, however, a complete blind spot had developed where his elder brother was concerned. If George demanded that he jumped, Stuart did so, without questioning the logistics or reasons. Sometimes, the boys managed to get themselves into scrapes, often needing our mother to extricate them. She would leave her home duties, bundle me into the car, so that she could rush up to school in response to a secretary's phone call, when one of her chicks was in trouble. Her patience with Stuart was unwavering.

George was more of a problem for her. She tried to be fair, but I suspect that her elder son would have tried the patience of a saint. Even when she repeated the misdemeanours to her husband, mother felt that they were losing a constant battle. George always showed remorse when our father spoke to him even if he did complain about his punishment, which usually involved being grounded or losing pocket money. Becoming more amenable and disciplined was not on George's agenda! He appeared to ignore all that had been taught by his parents and the vicar if the mood was on him.

Three weeks after the chicken hut incident, Dad caught him kicking the mesh as hard as he could and shouting abuse, using words that Dad had not heard since his war service. George was grounded for another week. Once home from school he was not allowed out, so he was unbearably grumpy. He was naturally, careful when the parents were around but he had a field day with us when they were not looking. Lizzie was as protective of Stuart and me as she was able and once homework was completed we stayed together in the sitting room. The board games and books had not been such good companions for a long time.

Being so much younger than the others, I was shepherded to bed by Mother Hen at 7 o' clock. About half an hour later, George often made his way along the landing from his bedroom to the tiny room that I inhabited whilst asleep. One horrifying night, George brought his glass of water with him. He ceremoniously poured it over my head wetting my hair. My pillow was also very damp. Somehow, ones own urine seeping into sheets is not as cold or uncomfortable. Who would have thought that such a small amount of water could cause so much unpleasantness?

George ordered me not to shout out and then stole stealthily back to his room. Within ten minutes mother had come up to check on me.

" Whatever has happened? Why are you so wet, darling?"

" George," I said with a simple smile.

Mother picked me up in her arms, took me along to the large family bathroom, wrapped a towel round me and rubbed me down as you might a thoroughbred.

" You poor love, my sweet," she cooed as she rocked me in her arms. " We'll take you to Lizzie in the sitting room whilst I deal with your wet bed ... and your big brother."

As I snuggled into the embrace of my big sister I was unaware of the reprimand my brother was receiving. Suffice it to say, he did not try that trick again! When I was fetched by Mum, she carried me back to my room, where she placed me in a freshly made bed. The sheets and pillow cases smelled like a spring morning and were soon a burrow for me to snuggle into for a peaceful night. As I got older, George only occasionally teased me. I fear this was possibly because he had more exciting schemes to plan.

By the time George was sixteen he had become more autonomous. Stuart was ripe for the picking and easy gathering because they travelled to school together on the bus. This old vehicle rattled along the country lanes, collecting pupils of secondary school age to take them into the town which lay about six miles north east of our village. Lizzie kept with her girl friends who were scattered around the seats but George and his domineering mates commandeered the back seat. When Stuart started at the Grammar School and had to take the necessary journey, he stayed with his friends at the front of the bus. By the end of the second week George had insisted that he joined him on the prized back seat.

When Lizzie recounted to Mum why the driver had stopped the bus, it became apparent that Stuart had behaved appallingly. He had stood on the seat, blocking the driver's view out of the back window, sung a dubious song, shouted, guffawed (with others joining in and adding to the insult by cheering), absolutely refusing to behave. The driver had stopped at a telephone kiosk, phoned his depot and the pupils were left stranded as though on an island. Eventually, the boys' school's deputy head had arrived on the scene, escorted Stuart and George off the bus, appeased the driver (who took the children on to their respective schools), ordered George into the passenger seat of his car and put my younger brother into the back with our sister, who was too upset to allow the deputy to take Stuart away without her in attendance. Mother was summoned to the school.

By the time we arrived, Stuart was a gibbering wreck, Lizzie was sitting in a corner with silent tears streaming down her cheeks and George was being entertained by the Headmaster. Stuart was invited by the deputy head to recount his sins to his mother but found himself tongue-tied, so Lizzie supplied the words. Our poor dear mother could hardly believe what she was hearing.

" Why?" she asked, turning to her younger son.

" It was George, of course," answered Lizzie softly.

" What does that mean?" asked the deputy head.

" He always persuades Stuart to misbehave. Stuart thinks it's big to do what he says."

" O.K. Lizzie," interrupted mother, " we get the picture. I think I'd better get you to school. What are you intending to do with Stuart?" she asked, turning her attention to the interrogator.

" We'll keep him away from the other boys today. Perhaps you could come back at the end of the day to collect your sons so that they are not on the bus. I suspect the Head will be dealing with George. He's older and should be more responsible."

" Certainly. Thank you. I'll be back at four. Come on Lizzie."

Mum hoisted me on to her hip and we took my big sister to her alma mater.

We had no idea what the Headmaster was saying to George, but mother fretted about it all day. She even fed herself my boiled egg instead of giving it to me once she had decapitated it.

" Oh I'm sorry, darling. Whatever was I thinking of? I'll make you another with some lovely soldiers, eh?" she asked with a smile.

Who was I to argue? I wasn't exactly 'frightened' of her, but I had a healthy respect, particularly at problematic times. Nowadays, with the use of the mobile phone, I expect she would have contacted our father, but in those days the man of the house was not expected to be interrupted at work unless there was a disaster. Mother decided that the latest escapade of the boys did not qualify, so we were all safely ensconced in the large kitchen when Dad arrived home.

I ran to him and he picked me up as usual, carried me towards Mother and planted a kiss on her head which was his usual practice. He then looked at the worried faces of his offspring.

" Why do I sense that there's another problem?"

" It's..." started George.

" I think I'd better tell Dad, don't you dear?" interrupted Mother.

When she had related the events, Dad dismissed us to the sitting room whilst he went upstairs to wash and change, leaving our mother to complete the preparations for dinner. It was her delicious shepherd's pie with greens and carrots from the garden and thick, tasty gravy. No shepherd's pie has ever tasted as good as the pies we had when I was a child. Now why is that? Do I over spice my culinary dishes or is it that the salt sergeant has influenced how much is used in preparation of the dish?

We did not need arguments in our house. I think Dad's word was the ultimate law and we were all wary of Mother's wrath, accompanied by her withering look!

After our delicious supper, Lizzie and I were sent into the sitting room to read and play together. We had a special game at this time. Lizzie was a would-be adopter who came to an orphanage for a child and she always chose me. On the way home she took me around the shops to buy me new clothes and toys before we arrived at the big house on the corner which had a huge garden for me to play in. As far as I can remember, there was no mother or father, no brothers or sisters and no pets, - until I begged for a cat to cuddle. It was always the same play that was acted out, but as we rarely had the opportunity to be alone without the boys it was always fresh and exciting.

I never found out what was said to the boys, but only Lizzie was allowed on the bus to school and Mother was forced to take them each day in the car. I, of course, travelled in the back, usually with Stuart. I think Mother realized that George would kick, tease or pinch me if we were next to each other.

For a time, the boys were subdued, which was a welcome change in the house. I presume George was banned from his bike as he always seemed to be working at the kitchen table. I think he was preparing for his exams. I avoided him as much as I could. When you are pre-school, you are too young to judge people's moods. It was only when I was older that I was able to choose with whom I shared a table. When it's your brother who is creating the tension it is not as simple!

CHAPTER 4

Fetes worse than...

Peaches and cream, Romeo and Juliet, Wallace and Gromit, cheese and biscuits. You would think that friends and village life would be linked together. After all, life in a village is depicted as idyllic and we all know that friendship is priceless.

However, it is more often ' Venus and Mars'. That's not saying that it's a male versus female situation; more a dominant personality vying against another person who is attempting to gain the upper hand. This, in turn, leads to squabbles and disharmony. Disharmony can lead to scandal. Scandal is often the precursor of gossip. Village life is full of it! 'Midsomer's Murders' may be exaggerated, but relationships there have been well observed. In our village, there were many strong people in different walks of life. This was sometimes evident in the daily routine of our village and there were occasions where voices were raised or people had a difference of opinion. Generally we felt that life had treated us well and I am certainly pleased that I grew up in Horbury Markham.

The Village Green was all that a picture postcard required. Luscious, succulent blades of grass were, in the summer, trimmed to perfection for activities demanded of such a communal space. Surrounding houses complemented the location; some small and compact, others large and grand, some terraced, others detatched. All had well-tended gardens; many being the handiwork of our own village gardener, Bert. In the 1950s it was usual to have a country garden at the front of the house, with hollyhocks, rose trees and jasmine. These were the gardens that provided scent and visual enjoyment for all the residents of the village.

The kitchen garden for vegetables and herbs was at the back of the house, viewed only by the occupants through the kitchen window. The Harper's gardens surrounded the house as they were on all sides, and walls and hedges (the bane of Mr. Harper's life, as they seemed to grow so quickly and were forever needing pruning) shielded their home from prying eyes. The children were often seen playing in the side garden on a bright Saturday morning or during school holidays. They knew that it was a corner of Paradise.

As Ray Davies said some years later when asked about his work, 'Village Green Preservation Society,'

"It was made to make a statement about village life amidst the turbulence of the late 60s. and it was a plea to the nation to hold firm to the qualities which had made it great."

It was many people's dream to own a house or cottage in a village. Of course, everyone seems to know everyone's business, so if you are a sharer, life in a village is idyllic; if not then it could probably be torture!

The Summer Fete brought the village people together. It was always held on The Green and I do not remember it ever being rained off, although I expect the Church Hall would have come on as substitute if the weather was inclement. Everyone in the village was involved in some way, be it moving tables, manning a stall, counting money after the event, providing refreshments, publicising the fete, or just attending and spending some money.

Our family loved to be involved. Dad always entered his vegetables in the 'Best of Show' tent; tending and preparing them for shows being an art in itself. Onions have to be the same shape and size as the others on a string and beetroot have to be the same size and shape as each other on a plate. Parsnips and carrots have to have the same diameter, length and shape, as do runner beans and spring onions. We had to gently scrub potatoes, swedes and turnips which, (yes, you've guessed) had to be the same shape and size as each other! Stuart loved preparing these vegetables as the water was really muddy and gritty, which he thought was great fun. Dad often won prizes for his exhibits, but they rarely came back home with him. They usually found their way to a couple of poorer families who lived in the village. Dad often took vegetables round to them when he harvested.

"Mrs. Cox makes a good onion, or parsnip, or pea, or vegetable soup for the family," he'd smile.

Mrs. Wells from the Baker's took spare bread to the needy families and I am sure that they benefitted from Marcus the

Butcher's contribution of meat. Mum had to enter cakes and home-made jams (blackberry and strawberry flavours) in the produce section at The Fete, but she always brought home cakes and jams as we ate a lot of that sort of thing in the 50s.

As a family we were responsible for 'Splat the Rat' and 'Pin the tail on.' For the former, Dad had made the tunnel and splatter in his shed and Mum had stuffed an old stocking with scraps of material to make the rat. Lizzie had not liked the fact that it had no eyes, nose or mouth, so mum sewed buttons on the 'rat' and gave it an embroidered mouth, producing a delightful smile throughout its splattering adventures. In later years, Stuart felt that the rat needed ears, so Mum obliged again by using up some pieces of felt that were left over from a circular hat that she had made for a winter wedding outfit. George named the rat 'Fred' which led to the demise of the 'Splat the Rat' notice and the birth of one which read 'Smack Fred Dead.'

'Pin the tail on' had started its life as 'Pin the tail on the donkey.' This, however, was far too specific for Lizzie and George and they suggested that the animal should be changed annually. Sometimes the tail had to be pinned onto a pig, sometimes a horse, or a cow, as well as 'the year of the donkey.' The change was appreciated by the village children, if not by the older, more traditional members of the community.

Gladys Joyce organised the fetes. She was a marvellous woman; full of enthusiasm, hard work (beyond the call of duty), ideas and her own opinion. This sometimes led to disharmonies and ill feeling. In all fairness, she made a wonderful fist of everything with which she was involved, and the only way to deal with her was to approach her with respect and wariness. Some people had fallen out with her, refused to mend disagreements and would not help with the Fete, but our mother suggested that if we "trod on eggshells" with her all would be well.

When I first heard this phrase, I envisaged that we must collect all the broken eggshells and put them between her and us before we spoke to her. I drew a picture of it which I shared with Lizzie, who laughed and said she hoped that this was only an image. I admitted that I didn't understand what mother meant. Lizzie explained.

"If someone is difficult, you have to be careful around them or it could cause more problems. 'Treading on eggshells' is an old expression that means you have to watch what you say to some people because it could lead to trouble. It's sometimes better to keep quiet rather than say what you feel."

" Does that mean they will be careful with you?"

"Oh no. They don't seem to realize how awful they are! But, they can cause more trouble than you would want, so it's always better to be careful with them."

I decided that this was a very odd state of affairs and that when I grew up, I wouldn't 'tread on eggshells'. I could not imagine that life is like that. As the years went by, I learned that sometimes it is better to keep one's own counsel.

However, I also learned a salutary lesson. Some people found me abrupt and were wary of me! It was a great surprise as I always imagined I was easy going. Perhaps that was the perception that Gladys Joyce had of herself!

CHAPTER 5

TRUTH WILL OUT

Why are mothers always surprised when their children lie to them? Tell them the truth to the question, 'Whatever made you do that?' and Mount Etna erupts.

The lie was invented for children. It could ease a conscience, cleanse a thought and ensure that no responsibility would be taken for an action. An imaginary friend is the best excuse ever invented (two are even better!)

' It's Yeh-yeh's fault,' ' Tunti did that,' or ' I told them you'd be cross, but they wouldn't listen!'

When these friends become part of the family their presence creates extra work. Places have to be set at the table, crocks and cutlery have to be put out, collected, washed up and dried before being replaced in the cupboard ready for the next meal. How people with small tables manage, I'll never know! Nowadays the dish washer must make the after eating tasks less arduous, but when I was small there were no such labour saving devices. Families are very tolerant of small children's whims until the child becomes older. Then such fantasies are not allowed.

Stuart had reached the age when our father would wrinkle up his nose and raise his eye-brows at some of the lies that accompanied an unacceptable deed. When the dog chased Farmer Hopps' sheep, Stuart told Dad that Bob had slipped his lead. Like so many parents Dad knew instinctively that this was a lie and suggested that Bob may have had a little help.

"Oh no, Dad," lied Stuart.

"I'd rather you told me the truth, my boy. Always better to face up to our mistakes," he smiled.

At first Stuart had remonstrated with him, but our father picked at the situation like a dog with a bone, eventually making Stuart admit that he was guilty of giving Bob his freedom amongst the sheep.

I don't remember Lizzie ever being in trouble because she had told a lie. She argued that once one lie was started, others had to follow to cover the first one. Although she was a very good person ('good as gold,' mother would tell anyone with a listening ear when she talked of her 'chickens'. Funny, that she meant us. Dad's chickens lived in the hen-house at the bottom of the garden and we children were 'the young uns') Lizzie was never 'holier than thou' or even ridiculed by her peers. She oozed kindness and consideration. Everyone automatically loved her which was why she was always class representative at school and later, Head Girl.

No wonder I tried to emulate her!

Unfortunately, I was not as pure as she was...Perhaps it was because I was from a different gene pool. If truth be told, I learned what buttons to push with our dear mother; I secretly enjoyed her screams and threats that she dealt out to my brothers. She only ever picked me up and laughed when I pushed my luck with her - until the day I lied about the broach.

Dad had left for work, my siblings were at school and Mum was pegging out the washing. I stole into my parents' bedroom, opened mother's jewellery box and found the most precious blue butterfly broach that had once belonged to Grandma Smith (our maternal grandmother). Mother wore it on special occasions. Its delicacy was always admired. The colour and alluring texture had not passed me by.

Jewellery is bewitching. It has a shape all of its own. It sparkles. It seduces. It begs to be touched, worn, loved. 'Thou shalt not covet.' A commandment so difficult for members of the human race. So many adults desire to keep up with the Joneses in homes and gardens. At the tender age of four I wanted, indeed needed, a beautiful, blue butterfly which nestled in the folds of my mother's jewellery box.

As I took the most precious piece out of its comfy place I remember my heart beating as hard as when I had fallen in the garden and hurt my knee, which had to be lovingly soothed and plastered. I cradled the tiny insect in the palm of my hand, closed its new home gently and tiptoed back to my own bedroom.

Now what? I could not wear it for fear that Mother would notice. It had to be hidden from view or else anyone who entered my room would see its shiny surface. I had an idea. I pinned the broach onto Teddy's fur; a difficult task for a four year old and a stubborn toy's covering. I admired him and showed him his adorned torso in the mirror. He smiled with satisfaction as I returned him to his place of honour on the counterpane and went back downstairs.

Within an hour, the crime had been discovered. Parents are such good detectives. They should probably help the police to solve all crimes.

"Judith," called my mother from the top of the stairs. "Come up here darling."

I wondered if I could ignore her request, but when I heard the demand, "Now!" I decided to climb the steps to the gallows.

My mother was clever. No obvious question like, "Why has Teddy got my broach pinned to him?" or "Have you been in my jewellery box?" but a smiling remark, "I didn't know that Teddy had a beautiful butterfly broach like mine."

"Umm, err."

"I bet it's hurting him pinned like that."

"He likes it Mummy," I intervened.

"How do you know? Did he tell you?"

"No....Tunti said."

"Oh! Tunti knows does he?"

"Yes. He likes broaches too."

Mother continued to remove Blue Butterfly.

"I think it would make a good friend for the one that was Grandma Smith's don't you? Come on, we'll take it to the box shall we?"

She took hold of my hand (quite firmly as I recall) and we went into the parental bedroom. As she opened the box, her eyes widened and she turned to me saying, "Grandma's broach isn't here. Do you know anything about that?"

"No Mummy," I replied, quivering in my shoes.

"Judith. You must be honest with me. Did you take it?"

"No. It was Tunti."

"Oh. And why was that?" Her tone was becoming more menacing.

"He thought that Teddy would look nice with a broach on."

"Are you sure that it wasn't you Judith? Are you sure that you didn't want to look nice?"

"No, no, Mummy. It wasn't me."

I was panicking. What would she do? Would I be smacked? Banished to my room? Forced to forego lunch? Miss my pocket-money? George always had his pocket money stopped when he did wrong.

"Please don't lie to me, Judith," my mother pleaded.

"It was Tunti," I persisted, waiting to see her reaction.

She sat on the edge of the bed, covered her eyes and cried. Not gently, not howling, but sobbing, her shoulders and body heaving as though she had heard dreadful news.

I was devastated.

Why had this lie not led to admonishment?

Why had my sin made her so sorrowful?

I crawled onto her knee and put my little arms round her neck.

" Don't cry Mummy. Please don't cry."

She composed herself.

"Lies are so destructive, Judith. One lie always leads to another and that destroys a pure heart. You MUST NOT do this again. I know jewels are must haves, but not if they belong to someone else; that's stealing. We don't do that do we?"

I realized that I had not admitted my crime overtly, but it had not been necessary. Mother's weapon on this occasion had been tears. She had had no reason to shout or scream at me. Her tears had poured down as her hurt had struck.

Parents are forced to use different tactics for different personalities within a family; a concept difficult for their brothers and sisters to appreciate at an early age. Had my mother been manipulative or genuinely bereft that her youngest child had chosen to blame the imaginary friend rather than face her misdemeanour squarely? Whatever the tactic, her tears had been effective. I see the event vividly. Even now, white lies are difficult for me, unless they are to help someone else. I think I blush as I say them so I'm sure people know anyway!

This act of 'Blue Butterfly Broach borrowing' had resulted in me lying AND stealing. The thought led me into joining Mother in sadness. Sobs and tears showed my sorrow for my sin.

My mother cuddled me to her. I was forgiven. I vowed not to lie to her again. I would try to be like Lizzie. I wondered if something like this had ever happened to her?

CHAPTER 6

VILLAGE CARS

There were few cars in the village. Our father had one because of his work. He was a pharmacist in nearby Bristol, who met many people when they went into the shop with a prescription which needed to be dispensed. Mother had been a secretary to one of the solicitors and remained in the job until she and Dad married. They had attended the same Presbyterian church in Bristol and got to know each other more intimately when Mavis and George Broad had started the Fellowship of Youth. After their marriage, Mavis and George had remained friends of our parents and were godparents to George and Lizzie.

Dad's Humber Snipe was his pride and joy (after the family and his chickens) and he kept it as clean and shiny as a new pin. The inside was always neat and tidy, like his study. Presumably chemists have to be precise and orderly so that they give out the correct medication that correlates with the doctor's prescription.

Horbury Markham's village doctor had a Rover 90. If we saw it parked outside one of the houses, we all knew that a patient was too poorly to walk down to his surgery, which was at the front of his house. As he served other villages, the surgery had restricted opening hours, but Mother taught us that we were privileged to have him living in our own village. Once a month, she and Mrs Holmes, the doctor's wife, spent an afternoon together sewing garments for an African mission that the church supported. In later life, I wondered why they had not included other ladies in their sewing 'circle' but I suspect that my mother's no nonsense approach was too off-putting for those with a more delicate disposition.

Farmer Hobbs had a long, grey, imposing Jaguar. It was the envy of the males in our family and George begged our father to buy one.

"We don't have that sort of money," laughed Dad.

"Just be thankful that we have our Snipe, George," added Mum, "we are lucky to have a car so soon after the war".

"Why?" asked Stuart.

" So many people lost everything, including cash, homes and the necessary where-with-all to make a decent living," she replied.

"And some lost loved ones, which is far worse than possessions," added Lizzie, my lovely sister. She always thought about people and was sensitive to others' needs. I knew even then that she would become a beautiful adult.

"That's right, my darling," said Father, " we are a lucky lot. Praise God."

Our vicar rode a Raleigh bicycle around the village. He had a wicker basket at the front, which was always laden with books, papers and jars of home-made jam or preserve that he acquired on his visits to parishioners. His wife had been very ill three years before I was born, so everyone had rallied round him in order to ensure he stayed with them. Margaret had been a vivacious woman who had run the school with enthusiasm and kindness. Now she was only able to manage gentler pursuits like the ' knitting circle'!

The trades people who brought supplies to the village ran small Standard vans. Inside these were lots of goodies for people to buy. The fish van was driven by a jolly, red-faced man who blew a piercing whistle when he arrived. He came round on a Friday morning and I think that everyone in the village bought from him; most people in those days ate fish on Fridays and it wasn't only Catholics that abstained from meat in respect for Christ's death. However, I think it was tradition rather than belief that led this trend.

The tall, thin, dark-haired man who delivered the groceries announced his presence by blasting his horn. This would always make the dogs bark, but it made our mother rush around to find her purse and basket so that she could hurry out to make her purchases 'before the masses'.

The baker delivered bread three times a week. He carried his bread in a huge basket which he took from the back of his green Morris van. 'Hudson's Bakeries' was painted in white letters on the side and there was a painting of it and Mr Hudson alongside the words. I always thought that the van looked as enticing as the bread and cakes that were sold. Mum only bought cakes on a Friday as she always baked a fruit cake for Sunday to cut at for the rest of the week. Sometimes we had the coveted sponge cake but it did not keep as well as one with fruit in it, so this was normally only baked when we had visitors to tea. The grandparents often dropped by but they did not count as visitors, so usually had a slice of 'Beryl's beautiful fruit,' as it was known by the family, with a cup of tea.

I liked it when the coal man delivered. He had a horse and cart to pull the bags of coal. People rushed out when the horse deposited its manure on the road because it was an added fertilizer for the roses. We always thought that one of our neighbours, old Mr Joiner, lay in wait for him because he often managed to get his shovel to the spot before anyone else. His roses were magnificent. He always won prizes with them at the village fete, but once it was over he would bring a bunch of roses to our house for our mother. The fragrance filled the air for a few days until mum replenished the vase with other flowers from the garden.

Our milk was delivered daily by a cheerful man called Thomas. He drove a milk float which rattled round the village roads.

We also had a mobile library which was a large van laden with books. As it came during the day my brothers, sister and father hardly saw it, but Mother had excellent taste and nobody seemed disappointed by her choice of book. The library lady was lovely to me and always chose appropriate material for my mother to read out loud.

The knife grinder came round each month in his van, which held great fascination for us all if we were about; it seemed an art in itself. The knives were VERY SHARP once he had set his grinder to the task, so children were not allowed near them.

Aunty Jane had a mobile butcher in her village, but we had Marcus in situ so there was no need for mobile meat!

We had a daily paper delivered by a young boy whom Lizzie knew from school. He was obviously interested in her as he always blushed when he saw her in church, but she showed little interest in him. Although, I think it was he who took her for a walk when she was older and talked about budgerigars and motor-bikes; enough to put off any self-respecting girl!

Mr and Mrs Green were our elderly neighbours. When Mr Green went into a home for the elderly, his wife moved away to live with her daughter and their house was put up for sale. One day, on the way home from being dropped off by the school bus, George noticed that there was a Ford Anglia outside the Greens' old house.

"I expect it's the new people," said Lizzie, who had heard Mum telling Dad that the new owners of the house lived abroad and that they had let out their new acquisition.

"We'll take a closer look at the weekend," promised George.

"Oh, a stake-out," shrieked Stuart. "I love that."

"What's that?" I asked.

"We wait quietly and watch from somewhere that hides us from view of the person we're investigating. It can be great fun," explained Lizzie.

"We usually know who lives in the house, so this will be more exciting," joined in Stuart.

"Oh!" I said, not really understanding what was intended or why it was necessary. But, I had already learned to be careful about the questions I asked if George was involved in any plan, particularly if it had been initiated by him. Even at the age of three and a half, I understood the meaning of 'treading on eggshells.'

CHAPTER 7

STAKE-OUT

As the weekend approached, Stuart could hardly contain his excitement.

"What's wrong with you, dear?" asked our mother, "You're very twitchy. And, DO be careful with that drink or else it'll be over the floor, instead of in you."

"It's because it's the weekend Mum,"answered Lizzie for Stuart.

"Oh. Is there anything special on then?"

"Not really," interjected George. "It's just nice not having to go to school. After all, there aren't any matches at school this Saturday, so we shall have a full weekend at home for once. We can probably play out a lot if the weather stays fine."

Clever boy! Always able to think quickly and change the subject into something as mundane as the weather.

Mother immediately answered, "Yes. It would be good for you to be able to get out. Perhaps you'd like to take a picnic and go into the woods?"

"Oh lovely!" said Stuart.

"That would be nice," added Lizzie.

"Can I go too?" I asked.

"Of course, darling; if Lizzie promises to take special care of you."

"No problem," answered Lizzie. "Come along Judith, we'll go and sort out what clothes you'll need."

My brothers and sister had learned how to extract themselves from difficult situations. I'm sure Mum had no idea of our weekend plans and I expect she was envisaging us being amongst the bluebells and primroses whilst we ate our picnic. I hope she wasn't expecting a nosegay of wild flowers!

Lying on your front is rather uncomfortable when you reach the age of fifty plus, but the child's body is as flexible as an Italian soft leather shoe; being in this position is as easy as lying on the back or side.

My brothers and sister enjoyed this activity, having involved themselves in 'stake-outs' on previous occasions when they had deemed it necessary. A new car, new inhabitants, visitors to neighbours and monitoring the development of The Parnells' road to divorce had all been necessary stake-outs.

Naturally, George's organisation was perfect. He had chosen a spot that was secluded, but would not rouse suspicion if we were spotted, so that we could observe the new people in Mr and Mrs Green's house. The trees along the boundary were a barrier as well as an acceptable place to play, as there were no flowers or vegetables growing there.

George insisted that I lay at the end of the line, next to Lizzie.

"You must not talk or wriggle around or else you may be heard and that would spoil the whole effect," he said sternly.

Who was I to argue with him? I nodded meekly and Lizzie placed a protective arm around me.

"Don't speak so harshly to her George. I'll look after her."

"You make sure you do as George says," butted in Stuart. "He knows what we should do, don't you?" he added admiringly, smiling at our older brother.

"Of course," replied George smugly. "Now," he continued, " no more talking and lie quietly."

"What if I need to wee?" I asked tentatively.

"I'll look after you," comforted Lizzie.

"I hope you went before we came out. I thought you might be trouble."

The eggshells were being broken again. I realized I had to keep quiet and wait for the instructions from my disagreeable brother.

Perhaps adults have less tolerance for twigs and grass pressing into their bodies. I don't remember the exercise being uncomfortable or unpleasant in any way. When I eventually needed to go home to relieve myself, I nudged my sister, who stood up quietly in one movement, put out her hand and we slid away from the boys, across the lawn and through the side door.

"You're back early," said Mum.

"We need the lavatory," replied Lizzie.

As I skipped to the bathroom I heard Mum asking, "Are the bluebells and primroses out yet?"

"Oh, we didn't go to the woods," smiled Lizzie. "We're under the trees at the side of the house."

"Well, that's as good a place to have a picnic as anywhere else I suppose."

Lizzie went to the bathroom when I came back into the kitchen.

"Having a good time?" Mum asked, as she brushed off a stray twig.

"Oh yes, it's lovely."

"Have you had your picnic yet?"

"We haven't had time."

Fortunately, Mother didn't probe deeper.

"Oh. Well, tell George you ought to eat now or else there won't be enough time between meals."

"What are you cooking?" I asked.

"We'll have a tasty beef stew with lots of vegetables."

"Oh good," I replied, as Lizzie returned.

"Come on," she called to me. "Let's get back."

"I've told Judith that you ought to be eating your picnic now. There's stew tonight and you need a gap between meals."

"O.K." smiled Lizzie, running across the room and planting an affectionate kiss on Mother's cheek.

"You didn't say anything, did you?" asked Lizzie, as we made our way back to our brothers.

"No!" I replied indignantly.

"Good girl," she smiled. "We'll persuade George that we should open our picnic now, shall we?"

George took no persuading. Like all growing boys, he and Stuart had hollow legs and they probably ate my share of the meal as well as their own.

We had to abandon eating when we heard a door bang. A man emerged. In Lizzie's notes on the day she records:

'He was quite old, but probably not as old as Mum and Dad, wearing a smart suit with a shirt and tie and highly polished shoes. He looked pleasant. No sign of woman, child or pet.

Stuart sneezed. He turned and raised his hand. (G furious with S). Man went off in car. Ate picnic. G moaned at S because Man saw us.'

I'd enjoyed the adventure of being on a stake-out with my brothers and sister, but was aware that George's reactions always spoilt a day. If only we could have stood up to him, I'm sure it would have been better for everyone. Although, I don't think I thought about that at my tender age; it's only with hind sight that it seems the case. We made two more stake-outs and both went smoothly. The man did not appear to leave the house, played very loud music and seemed to be somewhat of a recluse. We really did not know any more about him than we did when the stake-outs began.

Chapter 8

Coronation Year

1953 was an iconic year. Elizabeth, the elder daughter of King George V1 and his wife Elizabeth was to be crowned the Queen of England. Her coronation was to be televised, so after much deliberation, my parents decided to purchase a small ten inch Cossor television from John Mayer's Electrical Goods in Bristol.

There was great excitement on Saturday 7th March, when the television was delivered and installed in our sitting room. John Mayer himself brought it and explained its operation. Of course, one had to get up and down to adjust the volume, contrast and vertical hold once the set had warmed up; it took an awfully long time-almost five minutes which seemed like a lifetime when I was young. Over the months, our father became increasingly frustrated with its ways so he made himself his own Heath-Robinson device. He attached a sucker on to a garden cane so that the former could be stuck onto the contrast knob of the television in order to control the picture quality from his arm chair. Naturally, George enjoyed operating it if Father was not with us and woe betide any of us if we tried to become the operator!

As Children's television was limited it did not dominate our lives, so we still played outside or occupied ourselves with indoor activities. I have to admit that I really enjoyed 'Andy Pandy' and 'Muffin the Mule.' In fact, my aunt gave me a tiny metal Muffin the Mule which I cherished for years as it lived on a window ledge in the bedroom. I sang along with the songs and my mother became Annette Mills during the day when we did the household chores. Maria Bird narrated the story of Andy Pandy who lived in a picnic basket. I loved Andy Pandy's friends Teddy and Looby Loo almost as much as Andy himself. 'Here we go Looby Loo' was a favourite song of mine to accompany housework with Mother and I could often be found crying when it was time for Andy Pandy ' to go home' as he waved 'goodbye.' How clever of Freda Lingstrom to create such a character. He was obviously a powerful invention as the programme was revived and shown until 2005!

My brother's favourite programme was 'Robin Hood'; another story that never loses its appeal. After all, robbing the rich to pay the poor is something we all continue to admire-isn't it? Girls were not really catered for in the early days of television, so Lizzie had to enter into the throes of Sherwood Forest, cowboy territory in the Nevada desert, or Greyfriars School with Billy Bunter and his pals. She, therefore, often chose to immerse herself in literature rather than television trivia. Her favourite books were about the March family by Louisa M. Alcott, ('Little Women,' 'Good Wives,' 'Little Men' and 'Jo's Boys') which she frequently quoted. Somehow Lizzie managed to bring in quotations from Miss Alcott's works almost everyday. When we were asked to do jobs she would reply,'We'll work like bees and love it too, see if we don't-as L.M.A. would say.' Or, if Stuart was complaining about things being difficult to complete, Lizzie would quip, "Poor Stuart 'it's so hard I'm afraid to try," which usually made him try harder. If Mum and Dad were having a disagreement Lizzie would refer to it as ' a domestic drama,' which appears in the final sentence of 'Little Women' or if one of the dogs misbehaved it would be commented on" In L.M.A's words, 'oh the little villain!'"

Her favourite quotation was delivered seriously and softly, when one of us was complaining about friends. " Remember what L.M.A. said, she would start as we all sighed in unison, 'Good books, like good friends, are few and chosen; the more select, the more enjoyable.'" There was often a chorus by the time Lizzie had reached chosen, and I suspect we all often thought about the final phrase; I certainly cherished old select friends throughout my life.

The day Queen Elizabeth was crowned was a cold rainy one in June. The only things I can recall about the television coverage include The Queen looking as laden as the contestants in 'Crackerjack' when they earned cabbages for wrong answers as well as toys, her frightened look in case the crown should fall off and Queen Juliana of the Netherlands riding in an open carriage in spite of the rain. It was, I know, a memorable day for everyone because I was surrounded by happy smiles.

Chapter 9

A cause for concern.

Questions can lead you into trouble, as I discovered with George. If ever I wanted to ask anything that could not be answered by Mother I chose to refer to my tolerant sister Lizzie. I learned very quickly that George was irascible with me and that the only answer I would receive from him was a snap, a disagreeable grunt or a despicable look. Had I only had him to care for me I'm sure that I would have felt unloved and unwanted.

When the others were at school and Dad was at work, Mum and I did household chores and shopping. Betty Lord owned the village shop. One morning when we went in there, Betty told Mother, "The new chap that's moved into the Greens' old house came in yesterday."

"Oh yes I expect he finds it useful having a shop so near. Is he married?"

"Don't think so. But, that's not the point."

"Oh!" replied our Mother.

"He was asking questions," she said conspiratorially.

"I expect he wants to know things about the village-being new."

"Well...most of his questions were about the children in the village."

"Really? What sort of things did he want to know?"

" How old they were, what schools were around for them to go to. You know, odd things for someone to be asking really."

"Did you tell him about my brood?"

"Well... yes. They came into conversation."

"I suppose you mentioned that we had adopted Judith three years ago," Mum said resignedly.

"Well... yes. He was ever so interested-and understanding. Said it was brave to take on someone else's child."

"What did you say to that?" asked Mum sternly.

"I told him that Judith was growing into a lovely child," she said smiling tenderly at me. "The others adored her and that you and your husband were doing a wonderful job."

"Well. Thank you for that," replied Mum shortly. "Now may I pay for my goods? I have some baking to do."

Mother could always bring a conversation to an end when she wanted. Mum almost dragged me out of the shop. She seemed very upset by what she had heard.

When we got home, she deposited me at the kitchen table with a colouring book and went into the hall. I heard her pick up the telephone. On her return she said,

"Aunty Jane sends her love and a big kiss," planting a kiss on my cheek, "and says we'll see her very soon!"

Mother seemed calmer, but she picked me up and hugged me hard before beginning her domestic tasks.

The next afternoon, Aunty Jane arrived at our house. Mum pretended that it was a lovely, unexpected surprise, but in retrospect, I presume that it had been arranged the previous afternoon.

"Have you managed to get someone to collect the children from school?" asked Mum.

"Oh yes," replied Aunty Jane, "I can stay into the evening. But I must get back in time to kiss them goodnight. Do you think that Stan could take me back?"

"Of course, love. Thanks for coming. You're a star," smiled Mum.

"Anything for you," answered Aunty Jane, tenderly.

Their gentleness towards one another alarmed me. It seemed unnatural and I sensed there was a problem.

"I'll get us a cup of tea. Do you want a drink, darling?" Mum asked me.

"Yes please, Mummy."

"Take your colouring book and crayons into the sitting room and I'll bring your drink through to you."

I knew from Mum's tone that there was no point in arguing with her so prepared to leave the kitchen. I jiggled off the chair, picked up my book, dropped the crayons, which Aunty Jane picked up and carried for me and made my way to the sitting room. Soon after I was settled, Mum arrived with the milk and as she and Aunty Jane returned to the kitchen she dropped a kiss on my head and whispered tenderly, " Only for a bit my darling."

As a family we were always pleased to see our Aunt, Uncle and cousins. When my brothers and sister arrived home from school, they were disappointed that it was only Aunty Jane visiting. Dad was the only one not surprised to see her on his return from work. At the time we decided that grown-ups must discuss really interesting things once children have been put to bed. I wondered if they had stake-outs or if Dad trod gingerly around our mother as we all did? After all, she had a tongue as sharp as a needle pricking the soul of anyone who crossed her. He did not seem to be overcome by her manner and she appeared to be in awe of him. Lizzie told us that our parent's good relationship was the reason behind our happy family life.

Dad took Aunty Jane home (I expect it was more convenient to go with him than to catch a bus, but it meant that Dad had to go almost back to Bristol) and that meant he missed our evening analysis of the day. However, Mother was calm. She settled us all at the kitchen table with scones, butter and strawberry jam with milk to drink whilst we told her about our day. Although I had spent most of the time with her and she always knew about my day, Lizzie said I was to pretend that it was the usual evening chat so that she and the boys could hear what I'd done.

"Why was Aunty Jane here anyway?" asked George.

"She never comes by herself," added Stuart.

"And never on the bus!" exclaimed George.

"Why shouldn't she come over?" asked our Mother smiling gently.

"She is Mum's sister," added my thoughtful sister.

"Yes," added Mother warming to her daughter's support, "and we don't have much opportunity to talk without Dad and Uncle Jim."

"You had Judith. So how could you talk?" asked George.

" I coloured in the sitting room," I chimed in.

" Only while we had a cup of tea."

"Oh," said George, looking crestfallen.

He was always trying to make a point if the situation meant that I could be seen as a hindrance or nuisance.

"Anyway, drink up!" encouraged our Mother. "It's getting on and there's school again tomorrow."

She was so clever. We instantly knew by her tone and body language that the time for bed was upon us.

"Come on my little princess," she said addressing me and picking me up in her arms, " It's up wooden hill for you. Get yourselves sorted," she added to the others. "I'll come up in half an hour, so you'll have time to read."

"I need to talk to you about my prayers," said Stuart.

"Oh!"

"I'm beginning to wonder why we have to say them."

"Really! Whatever makes you say that?"

"I don't see any sign of a new puppy and I keep praying for one."

"Ahh. Perhaps a chat about prayers would be a good idea. I can surely spare a few moments once I've put Judith to bed. Meanwhile..."

"Come on Stu," said Lizzie, "George and I will listen for five minutes before we go up. Is that O.K. Mum?"

"I expect so. Don't let it be any longer!" she replied with a warning hint in her voice.

With that, she carried me to the foot of wooden hill and we counted our way to the top and struggled through the brambles into the bathroom. It was too late for a bath, so I was given a 'strip-wash' before cleaning my teeth, performing a final wee and scampering across the landing into bed. Teddy was waiting for me and he and I cuddled together while I said my prayers.

"God bless Mummy and Daddy, Lizzie, Stuart and George, Judy and Bob my lovely doggies, my aunties, uncles and cousins and make me a good girl. Amen."

We stayed in a cuddle while Mummy read Teddy and me a story and when we had been kissed goodnight we snuggled down together until Lizzie covered us with kisses when she came up. As far as I know, the boys never came into my room when they came to bed. Daddy was usually kissed downstairs, although he told us that he always looked in on us before going to bed at the end of each evening.

I don't think that any of us realized that this day was to be the start of a new chapter in our lives. Aunty Jane had come to the house on a surprise visit, Mum had cuddled me more tightly than usual, Stuart was questioning the power of prayer and we had all had a late night despite it being a school day the next morning.

CHAPTER 10

TEA AND MYSTERY

Starting a new life in a new house, new road, new town and new county is demanding. The new occupant of the Greens' house caused nosiness and speculation, unknown to the village for many years; probably since when my parents bought our house fifteen years before!

Needless to say, the Harper children were no exception to the inquisitive disposition adopted by the members of our village. How would new people fit in to the ethos of Horbury Markham? I fear we thought ourselves rather special and were suspicious of newcomers.

Our father was the first of the family to encounter the new member of our community. Dad met him in the local shop when he went to buy the necessary extra pint of milk one weekend. His excited shout preceded his Tigger-bouncing stride as he returned to the coop.

"Guess who I met in Mrs Lord's?" asked Dad, in a manner which invited response.

"Mrs Groom," suggested Lizzie.

"No..."

"Mrs Joyce," said Stuart, who had a soft spot for the kindly lady and often helped her with additional jobs at the village fete.

Dad shook his head.

"Mrs Lord, of course," said George triumphantly.

"No, Clever Clogs. She served me, as you well know."

"Well, go on love. Who?"

"Robert Halford."

"Who?" chorused the family.

"The new member of our community turns out to be called Robert Halford, our neighbour."

Being a kind soul, our Father had engaged the gentleman in conversation and discovered that he originated from London. He had been transferred to Bristol by his Insurance firm. On the walk up from the shop, Dad discovered that not having any ties, Mr Halford had decided to rent a house in a nearby village rather than live in the city. A young, single man must be richer than a man with a wife and family, so I expect that was why he was able to run his Ford Anglia. He told dad that he often caught the bus into Bristol when he was required to be at Head Office because driving was a bit of a nightmare in his opinion. That explained why the car was often outside the house. George had wondered why our subject of surveillance appeared to be often at home; whereas, in fact, he went out without succumbing to the luxury of always using his car.

Dad told us that he had suggested that Mr Halford could have a lift to town with him but he had refused because he did not have regular hours or destinations. Dad accepted this without question.

When Dad had finished telling us about his meeting with Robert, he suggested that we invite him to join us for a meal.

"It must be quite lonely for him, all on his own."

"He plays loud music," started Stuart.

"You can hear it when you pass the house," interrupted George, deciding that Stuart was saying too much.

"It's not really our cup of tea, is it?" added Lizzie.

" Oh. I didn't realize you went that way much," said Dad.

"When we go up to the woods," explained Lizzie.

"Or across to the Old Field," interjected Stuart.

"The weather's been just the ticket recently," added our weather expert, George.

No one expected me to participate in this exchange and I received a warning look from the others so I knew we were not going to own up to the 'stakeouts'.

"We'll invite him to Saturday tea. When we have eaten, the children can watch 'Whirligig' and 'Hopalong Cassidy' whilst we chat and get to know each other."

"O.K. That sounds a good idea," replied Dad.

When we had been dismissed into the sitting-room, Lizzie told me that I was a good girl to keep quiet about the 'stakeouts' and advised me not to mention them when Mr Halford came to tea.

Mother put a formal note through our neighbour's door on Monday morning and he responded with a formal acceptance to

Saturday tea the following day. Mother and I baked on Wednesday and made a big fruit cake, which was Dad's favourite, and small cakes which we iced and decorated with 'hundreds and thousands.' Dad was asked to buy a pork pie and six slices of ham from the butcher's shop in North Street before he came home on Friday. We had to tidy our rooms in case Mr Halford went upstairs (more of an excuse for getting us to tidy up, I suspect.)

On Friday morning, I had my first experience of cleaning cutlery. I expect it had been done before, but I was encouraged to play a part in the 'preparation for Mr H's baptism' as George had christened the Saturday tea party. I had to polish the cutlery so that it sparkled like the sun on the pond once Mum had cleaned and wiped the smelly 'Silvo' off the forks and spoons. It was fun to see my face reflected in the back of the spoon as it looked fatter than usual and changed shape as I turned the spoon round. But, I did not enjoy the task for long as it made my arms ache.

Once my brothers and sister had finished their homework on Saturday, we waited for the knocker to be rapped on our front door. When it came I felt my heart hammering against my chest. What would happen if this new person recognised us from our 'stakeouts'? Would we be discovered and hear our mother's wrath or our father's disapproval? By the time our visitor arrived all was in order. I need not have worried as our father had answered it with a welcoming smile and a handshake, bringing him into the kitchen where we were all assembled. Here was our subject of surveillance standing proudly before us. We averted the gaze and I prayed. Mother Hen stood with her brood lined up in front of the Aga and we were introduced. Mother looked benignly at Mr Halford as he held out his hand to the boys, Lizzie smiled and I hid behind my mother's skirts. Mr Halford smiled and was then invited to go through into the sitting room with Dad whilst she finished the final preparations for tea. Lizzie set the table, I passed the newly cleaned cutlery to her and my brothers were sent to wash their hands. It was truly amazing that they always had grubby palms! After homework, there was usually big blobs of ink from their pens which crawled their way up to their wrists like the tide encroaching the beach. Mum despaired of them!

Sharing a meal with a stranger is not easy for children. Small talk is not available in chicks' brains. Mr Halford, however, was accomplished in the art and there did not seem to be a lull in the conversation over tea. When eating was finished we were sent into the sitting room to watch our programmes, which allowed the adults to talk. I worried that Mr Halford did not know that he should tread warily with Mother in case he smashed eggshells.

Once he had gone Mother remarked to Father that he seemed to ask an inordinate number of questions.

"What's that mean?" asked Stuart.

"He was making conversation," replied Dad.

"Being nosy," sneered Mum.

"Now Beryl, we can't have that!" warned our Father. "Anyway, I think he's quite lonely, so we must make him feel welcome and at ease. He'll probably be in church tomorrow so remember your manners; smile and be polite."

"Anyway, you all did very well today," assured our Mother, as she finished clearing the table and changing the subject she asked, "Was Hopalong a good story?"

Stuart proceeded to tell her about it whilst George and Dad discussed a Maths problem that was worrying his eldest.

It was at times like this that I was glad that I was able to cling to Lizzie. She and I went to the sitting room and plumped up the cushions which the boys had lolled against as they hadn't been supervised by our parents. In later life I learned that some families only used the sitting room when they had visitors. The television was in ours, which was a luxury for most people, so the room had a different purpose in our lives. Three children at Grammar School also needed space to complete homework and if my brothers argued with each other they had to work in different rooms! I wondered how big families that only had one room and a kitchen managed.

When it was time for me to climb wooden hill, Mum supervised the activity with accentuated care, told me my bedtime story, held me tightly to her, told me she loved me and incorporated my safety into the prayers. I felt overprotected and a little anxious. Why was she behaving in such a clingy manner? I knew better than to question her actions and smiled as she cooed, "Sleep well my little one." She climbed down the hill back into the bosom of the rest of the family. After such an exhausting time (why is it that entertaining is so tiring?), I was soon dead to the world and in dream land, so had no awareness of the anxiety that had been caused to my parents by Robert Halford's visit. As we never discussed it I think Lizzie and the boys were also unaware. We never talked negatively about Robert when we were by ourselves, but we did not know that he was about to play a significant role in our lives.

CHAPTER 11

ELIZABETH'S DILEMMA

Elizabeth Malvern had a successful career as a lecturer at University College London after she had graduated from L.S.E. in July 1954. She had been headhunted and her employers had not been disappointed. When she left Grammar School she attended a finishing school in Switzerland and had 'gone travelling to gain experience in life' before attending university. She had met Alec in Switzerland and as his father worked in the city, his parents could afford to fund his trip abroad before he embarked on working 'for his living'. Whilst in Switzerland, Alec worked at one of the ski resorts as an instructor whilst Elizabeth, affectionately known as Eliza, worked in its restaurant. Although she enjoyed his company, she was alarmed by some of his ideas about politics and money that he expressed when the young employees met for breaks.

Nothing deterred her desire for him and she day-dreamed about what being kissed by him might feel like. After a month's flirtation, they brushed closely past each other one evening and Alec grasped Eliza's arm, saying,

"Meet me outside the main door after work?"

Eliza had nodded, knowing that her dreams were to be fulfilled.

At every opportunity they kissed and cuddled and eventually touching developed into them enjoying intercourse with each other. They embarked on a love affair which Eliza entered passionately. Alec was a handsome man and she felt good by his side or tucked under his possessive arm. Whenever they could, they met and made love, sometimes under the stars under coats to keep warm. Somehow, she never felt cold despite her scanty clothing left after their passionate fumbling.

On his return from Switzerland Alec's father had bought his son a 'small' flat and procured a job for him in his firm.

Elizabeth's parents lived on the edge of Epping Forest in Loughton. Her father was a wealthy business man who had wheeled and dealed in the import and export world. A hard man, whose wife was conscious of her disingenuous approach to her life with him. Bernard worked long hours in the city and Stella filled her life with coffee mornings, good works being an ardent member of the WRVS who served coffee, tea and biscuits in the hospital at Chingford three afternoons a week and meeting friends. She had been a good mother to her three children who had all left home. Her eldest, Stephen, was happily married to a pleasant woman who had given him two adorable children, both boys, aged seven and four. Michael remained a bachelor, although she knew that he had plentiful lovers. Both of their sons worked in law; Stephen, a good solicitor, had a partnership in a firm in Basingstoke, whilst Michael was a renowned barrister and often appeared for defendants in trials at the high court. Stella and Bernard were slightly disappointed in Elizabeth. However, they agreed to rent a small bed-sit in London for their daughter who decided to do shop work before entering university on her return from her travels abroad. They had met Alec and presumed that they were a couple. Naturally, they had no idea that their daughter and the charming, rich young man were already lovers.

On their way home, the Malverns thought about the joy of parenthood as they drove along after an expensive meal that Alec had insisted upon buying for them at the 'little restaurant' on the outskirts of London not far from where his intended in-laws lived. He loved Eliza with all his heart. She was not as convinced about her love for him.

With two homes that could be used as meeting places, Eliza and Alec saw each other most nights of the week. The former was working part-time in a book shop in Oxford Street, which she enjoyed and found reasonably rewarding but untaxing. As Alec was training in the 'Family Firm' he seemed to be able to do almost as he wished as long as he gave his father notice. This led to two very energetic, attractive young people with too much spare time on their hands and, as they were already sexually active, too ready to use their spare time and energy in making love as often as possible.

In the year before her university entrance (to her horror), Eliza became pregnant. She had been terrified when she found herself pregnant feeling that her father would be unforgiving and sensing that there was little love lost between her parents and Alec. Initially she thought that she would try to get rid of the baby but where would she start? She considered a 'back street abortion,' but had read that they could lead to unlimited complications including death which she was not ready to face. In the end she had confided in her friend Pat, whom she would trust with her life. Unfortunately, Pat was scathing when she heard and had not offered the support for which Elizabeth had hoped. She agreed to keep the information to herself, but advised her friend to tell her mother.

Eventually, after much soul searching, a three month pregnant Elizabeth had invited her mother to her flat in Leytonstone. Over their evening meal, Stella listened to the sorrowful voice of her only daughter revealing that she was unexpectedly going to make her a grandmother.

" Is it Alec's?" she asked.

"Of course!" replied Elizabeth, indignantly.

"What does he say?"

"He doesn't know."

"Why ever not?" asked Stella, incredulously.

"Look... I don't want to marry him and settle down."

"Well, are you still seeing him?"

"Until the end of next week."

"What's happening then?"

"I'm finishing with him."

"Goodness! He'll be devastated."

"Perhaps, but I can't keep seeing him."

Stella thought for a moment.

"O.K. So, what are you going to do about the baby?"

"I'm not sure. I might have it adopted."

"You can't do that! We'll bring it up."

"No Mum. Thanks but no thanks. Dad will make its life unbearable. Anyway, I don't want him to know about it."

"Oh, come on. That's unreasonable and almost impossible to get round."

"Not if we tell him that I'm going travelling again and I'll go to university when I get back."

"I'll have to sleep on that idea, my dear. I don't like deceiving your father...although I know that he can be difficult," Stella added.

"I'm sure you'll think of something Mum," replied her trusting daughter.

Stella decided that they should keep the news of the pregnancy away from Bernard at that moment and invent further travelling experiences for Eliza before her delayed entry into university. Bernard wasn't pleased to learn that another year's money was to go towards his little daughter's travels, but Stella was convinced that this plan was the lesser of two evils and persuaded him of the virtues of Eliza experiencing more of her 'grand tour'. In truth, Stella dreaded Bernard's reaction to him becoming the grandfather of a bastard. She had spent her life being careful about what, when and how she spoke of events and knew that keeping the knowledge of their daughter's pregnancy from her husband would not, in fact, be difficult. Their conversation was limited at the best of times. Bernard came home from the City late, ate his meal, drank his wine and dozed until Stella roused him for the late night news and his evening cocoa before they retired to bed. If they were entertaining, Bernard was a picture of bonhomie with everyone and few realized that the stolid marriage of the Malverns had any cracks or flaws. Keeping the news from her other two children was more difficult for Stella. It became easier when Eliza told her that she had arranged for the child to be adopted.

"So don't think of getting attached to the idea of becoming a grandmother again," she was advised by her strong willed daughter. "There'll be plenty of time for that."

"Oh well," thought Stella, " Perhaps it is for the best."

When Elizabeth gave birth in Whipps Cross Hospital, Stella was by her side, having told Bernard that she was visiting a sick friend for a few days. The tiny girl was just what Stella had hoped for in a grand daughter. She was, however, sad. She knew that Eliza had signed the necessary adoption papers and that this little baby would not be part of their family in a month's time.

Elizabeth had very mixed feelings cascading through her head. The baby that had kicked her and been a part of her during her pregnancy was now out in the big world. She wondered if she should let Alec know that he had a daughter, but as she had never admitted to being pregnant she thought it was best left unsaid. Poor Alec. He had been bewildered when she had finished their relationship so suddenly just before Christmas in 1949. In spite of constant letters and elaborate presents he had not been able to win her back. Elizabeth had told him that he wanted more from the relationship than she had been prepared to give; she was not ready for marriage or settling down and becoming a suburban housewife.

Elizabeth hardened her heart in preparation for surrendering her first born. The baby girl was perfect, but Eliza knew that she wasn't ready for motherhood and had been assured by the welfare officer that the baby would go to a good home.

"Have you named her?" she was asked.

"Yes."

"Would you like the adopting parents to keep the name which you have given her or choose one of their own?"

"I don't mind."

"Very well. You realize that you have two months to change your mind about the adoption?"

"Oh yes; but I shan't."

With this, the baby was taken away from her mother and given up to an unknown future.

CHAPTER 12

COMING CLEAN

Elizabeth tried not to think about her baby.

She flung herself into her academic life at university from 1950 just four months after giving birth. She avoided having any form of relationship with the men she met. As she became engrossed in the world of academia the image of her face faded. She graduated in 1954 and became a lecturer having been a leading light in debates at the L.S.E. Her career was up and running.

Poor Stella had not enjoyed the years which had passed since she witnessed the birth of her grand daughter and woke in the night from troubled dreams about the little baby girl. She began to feel very downhearted with her life. She began to lose weight and lost her ready smile and laugh. Even Bernard noticed that his petite wife was becoming morose and introverted. He began to show concern and questioned her about what was bothering her.

"Are you ill?" he asked.

"Of course not."

" I know that there's something wrong. You're always tearful and you've lost a lot of weight."

"I'm just feeling a bit down." She tried to fob him off but this time Bernard was more pressing with his questions.

"What's worrying you Stel?" he asked lovingly.

Stella burst into tears. Bernard crossed the room, put his arms round her and let her sob out the past years of heart ache. When she was calmer he asked again.

"What's bothering you, darling?"

"I'm sorry. I've kept something from you that I should have shared."

"Well, tell me now."

"I can't."

"Why ever not?"

"You'll be so angry."

" I see. Do you have to tread on eggshells with me, even after all these years?" He smiled.

"Well. It's difficult."

"Try me."

Stella pulled herself upright and twisted her damp handkerchief between her fingers. "Well you see..." she began.

"Yes?"

Stella took a deep breath. " Well...Eliza didn't do more travelling four years ago. She was pregnant."

"What?" he questioned in an appalled voice.

" I said you'd be angry."

"No. I think we'd better sit down with a drink and you can tell me all I need to know," he assured her encouragingly.

Stella recounted all the doubts and uncertainties of the dilemma which had faced Elizabeth. Bernard, uncharacteristically, listened to the story without interruption.

"Am I really so dreadful that you and Eliza are frightened to tell me the truth?" he asked incredulously.

"Yes. But that's not the real point," answered his long-suffering wife. " We have a grandchild and we don't know where she is or how she's getting on. Surely there's something we can do?"

"Does Eliza not want to see her?" asked Bernard.

"No. She's thrown herself into her work. But, Bernard, I want to know that she's happy. There must be something we can do."

" O.K." answered Stella's husband, patting her knee, " I'll think of something. Meanwhile, you must promise me that you'll never keep anything of such importance from me again. Surely you of all people, know that my bark is worse than my bite. I can't bear to think that you find me so unreasonable."

" I'll try to be better," assured Stella.

Bernard soon had an idea about how to go about finding his granddaughter and decided to set things in motion before sharing it with his wife. How amazing that there was a little girl out there who might look like him or have his colouring - or temperament. Goodness! Fancy nobody wanting to confide in him; was he really that awful? He had better be more restrained with his family. All right for the job but obviously not the approach to take with his loved ones. Wouldn't like to think of them having to 'tread on eggshells' before they told him anything of importance again. To think, a granddaughter would be about four or five now and his dear wife had borne this information on her own for all those years. Presumably his precious Eliza never talked about the baby and had refused to let Alec know that he was a father. In fact, had finished with him! Women could be very odd. Mind you, he hadn't much cared for the lad; wouldn't have liked him as a permanent member of the family. Insufficient spunk. Now, Gordon at work would be a fine son-in-law, if only Eliza would show some interest in men again. She must meet them at work. Perhaps getting pregnant had put her off. Anyway, this wasn't getting the baby a new bonnet; and he would like to do that! He turned his attention to the matter in hand and began to skim the telephone directory.

CHAPTER 13

WAYS AND MEANS

Private Investigators conjure up visions of American crime stories on British television or Humphrey Bogart in a black and white film. Bernard was old fashioned for the 1950s so he would have been completely at sea in the 21st century! However, he had eventually discussed his idea with Stella who had agreed that a professional should be employed to trace the whereabouts of their granddaughter. Stella had decided that they should tell Eliza of their intentions so they invited her over for a weekend. After their first meal, Bernard told Eliza why they wanted to see their granddaughter. Her reaction had not been positive.

Their daughter was furious that her mother had told her father about the situation which she had intended to keep strictly between the two of them. Stella was frustrated that her daughter could not understand her feelings towards her granddaughter. Bernard was bewildered by the animosity of his own flesh and blood.

"I know you didn't want me to be told about the baby, but I'm glad that your mother finally came clean."

"That's not the point," had been her retort, "It's the past. My life has moved on since then. I've put it behind me. I've got over the hurt and upset. I've a new life."

"But it's your baby. You're her mother."

"She has another mother and family now. PLEASE don't rock the boat for them all. She may not even know about me - or you."

"Your mother needs to know that she's alright."

"Oh I see. My mother's needs are more important than anything else. O.K. Go ahead. Find her. I don't want anything to do with it."

With this Elizabeth had stormed out of the room, gathered up her belongings, slammed the front door and driven into the night.

The following day Bernard had felt compelled to phone his beloved daughter to see that she was alright. Fortunately, Elizabeth was more philosophical the next morning and said she didn't want to row with her parents. However, she emphasised, she would not be part of the 'search for the grandchild.'

"Well dear, we decided to do it professionally so that nobody would get hurt."

"Oh. How do you hope that will work?"

"P.I.s know what doors to knock and how to get information out of people without too many hiccups."

"So, you say."

"Well. We've put it into the hands of a chap who seems pretty au fait and reasonable."

"Don't spend thousands of pounds on it, will you Daddy? It really isn't worth it and, as I said last night, it's all in the past."

"Yes I know that, but we'd be happier to know."

Elizabeth knew that it was no use arguing. Her father had always made his point and stuck to it.

"O.K. Dad. Good luck, if that's what you really want. I need to get on now. See you soon."

With that she rang off and her father decided that he could now tell his wife that all was now well with their daughter and that she had agreed to their plan.

It would work out. Perhaps they could even all be a big, happy family.

CHAPTER 14

SEARCHING

Finding someone who doesn't want to be found is a source of nightmares. What did Bernard have to go on? Only the name of his daughter (if she had registered the birth in her own name), the name of the hospital, and the date of the birth. May 1950. Stella could no longer remember the details. As she explained, she had tried to put the event out of her mind but always remembered it was May because that was the month of her friend's birthday; the excuse for her few days away!

He took what information he had to a Private Investigator that he had found in the London telephone directory. He and Stella had agreed that money would be no object. His delighted wife had explained that they would have spent pounds by now on a grandchild if they had only had contact with her. There seemed some sort of logic in this he supposed! He wanted Stella to be well again. She seemed to be recovering her old joie de vivre and ready smile. He hadn't realized how much he had missed her neglected welcome upon his return home from work. He had not really noticed her change of demeanour until it was too late. Presumably, it had been gradual. He was determined to give her more attention and not put all his eggs into the work basket. He began to think more about his children. What his poor daughter must have gone through! He would have supported her and yet she had thought that he would disown her. Perhaps she hadn't wanted Alec's child. All in all he was glad that they had never married. He presumed that Stephen was happy with his family; they always seemed jolly. Michael? Was he content to be on his own? He no longer spoke of a special woman but he was good looking enough to have amours. He really must have a man-to-man talk with him when they were next together. How could you chat about such matters? Stella usually made the conversation with the children. He wondered if there were other things that she knew about them and had never shared with him? Must make a point of talking to her more often after the children's visits had ended. He drew up in front of the Investigator's office.

Robert Halford agreed to do some research for them but did not promise prompt results. He explained that with the type of information which he had he would need to get special permission to access the hospital records, which would incur more expense than usual for his clients.

"Whatever it takes," assured Bernard. "This is very important to us."

After a month Bernard received a call from Robert Halford who invited him over to his office to discuss one of his ideas. Bernard suggested that Stella came too. Mr Halford explained that his investigations had led him to Bristol and that he believed that their granddaughter was living with a family in one of the nearby villages. He didn't wish to rock the boat so his idea was to rent a house in their village, which he had seen advertised in the newspaper, ask a few questions and take it from there.

Bernard and Stella could see that this might work and went home feeling excited but somewhat apprehensive.

"Oh I do hope that it will work out," enthused Stella, as they began to drive home.

"Yes dear," said Bernard, patting his wife's knee affectionately. "But let's not put too many eggs in his basket. We'll just try to wait and see."

She looked tons better these days. Bernard knew that he was being a more considerate husband and felt justified with his recent approach to life. This chap would make everything right and they could once again become the family that Stella needed. He vowed never again to get so engrossed in his work that he neglected the most precious possessions that life had given him.

Better not tell anyone about the search for the granddaughter; that would be breaking a trust that he had only just regained. Life didn't get any easier with age, did it?

As he turned into the drive of their home, Stella hoped that they would bring a granddaughter there to share all the luxuries she was experiencing. Bernard hoped that the child would see the results of hard work and sound investments.

CHAPTER 15

A POLICEMAN CALLS

I did not realize that when we succumbed to George's demands, we were learning the rudimentary rules of 'treading on eggshells'. When he was sixteen, Dad taught him to drive round the lanes near the village. The local policeman must have turned a blind eye because now I am sure that this was illegal! Giving a bully an opportunity to get behind the wheel is bound to lead to serious trouble.

By the time George was seventeen, he was full of his own achievements. He was successful at school, a hit with girls, handy with tools and imagined himself to be the best driver of a Humber Snipe in the county. In fact, he passed his driving test easily and begged Father for the use of the car at the weekend.

"Where do you want to go?"

"Only to take Stuart and Lizzie for a spin."

"Well I'd rather not come thank you," said Lizzie.

"It'll be fun," enthused Stuart, with eyes shining like stars.

"Could I come?" I asked in a shy voice.

"No," snapped George.

"I think you're too little my darling," smiled Mum.

"Far too little," added Dad, scooping me into his embrace.

After lunch on Saturday afternoon, George and Stuart set off in the car for their suggested spin. Lizzie had homework to do, Dad was tinkering in the shed, so Mother and I baked scones and fairy cakes in the kitchen. Later I noticed P.C. Holmes walk down the path at the side of the house but thought nothing of it. The next moment, my ashen faced father was standing in the doorway of the kitchen.

"Beryl," he whispered stepping across the space in a stride and encircling his much loved wife in his arms. He guided her to a chair and squatted on the floor in front of her.

"Holmsey has come with some news," he began.

"What? What?" snapped Mum realizing that it could only be frightful if Dad was behaving in this manner.

P.C. Holmes interjected. "It's the boys, Beryl."

"Has there been an accident?"

"Um. Yes...It's all under control and the boys have been taken to hospital."

"Oh goodness. Whatever's happened?" shook my mother.

Sensing something was dreadfully wrong I moved to her side and she picked me up and lovingly held me on her knee.

"Fetch Lizzie," ordered my mother turning to her devastated husband. "Tell me," demanded Mother of P.C. Holmes.

"They ran off at the road and hit a tree," replied the policeman. "The car's a complete write-off."

"I knew that car was bad news. What about my boys?" Mum pleaded.

"They're at the hospital so they're in good hands."

Dad returned to the kitchen with Lizzie. He had already told her that there had been an accident involving her brothers and she too was as pale as a lily as she moved towards our beloved mother.

"I'll take Judith," she whispered. "You and Dad go to the hospital."

With this I was handed over.

"Make sure she's in bed by seven. You've got your homework to finish."

"I'll wait up for you."

"O.K. But we've no idea how long we'll be. Let the dogs out into the garden. They'll have to do without their walk tonight," replied Dad. At the word 'walk' the dogs roused themselves. Dad patted them and commanded them to settle. Judy was old, but could manage a short walk around the garden but Bob needed longer sojourns and much more exercise. Mum and Dad hugged us, put on their coats and left Lizzie and I in the kitchen.

"Shall I get us a story and a colouring book. Then we'll get you ready for bed?"

"It's not bedtime yet," I protested.

"No, you're right," Lizzie replied. "We'll need to have tea before that. I'm sorry. I'm feeling a bit confused at the moment."

"Will the boys be alright?" I asked anxiously.

"Who knows? Make sure you mention them in your prayers before you go to sleep tonight," she replied. "Anyway, what story shall we have?" she asked, changing the mood.

"OOH... Let's have 'The cheeky boy'"

This was a story from Enid Blyton's 'The Teddy bear's Tail and other stories', which Lizzie had won as a class prize when she was younger. It was a much loved book in our house and had been resurrected when I joined the family. Lizzie smiled and fetched the book from the shelf in the sitting room. We cuddled up together in the large comfy chair which stood one side of the kitchen AGA, unaware of the drama that was unfolding in the hospital.

CHAPTER 16

A HEAVY PRICE

PC Holmes had driven as fast as he could safely go. He had seen the wreckage of the car and the crumpled bodies of the boys.

"Don't be too alarmed when you see your boys," he started.

"Why? What's happened to them?" demanded our mother.

PC Holmes knew that Beryl Harper was a terse woman and had to be treated with kid gloves, so he answered quietly,

"It was a bad crash. When you hit a tree, it's an immovable object and is unforgiving. The boys are badly hurt."

"Do you know more than you're letting on?" asked our astute father.

"Not really. They'll do as much as they can at the hospital. But, I don't want you to be unprepared."

"I don't think I want to speculate," retorted Mother. "Let's wait until we get there."

Our parents reported to Reception at the big hospital in Bristol, which dealt with all the emergencies and illnesses in the area.

"Come this way," said the Sister pleasantly as she led them into a room. "Doctor will be here in a moment."

My anxious parents waited in silence. Dad kept a protective arm round his wife, who leaned into his shoulder. At last a Doctor arrived. My father stood up and the Doctor put out his hand in greeting.

"Mr. Harper. I'm Dr. Hawes. Mrs. Harper," he added as he turned to Mother.

"Well?" she asked.

"I'm afraid it isn't good news. The driver has a fractured leg, arm and ribs."

"And Stuart?" asked Mum shakily.

"He is very poorly. He seems to have taken the brunt of the impact."

"Can we see our boys?"

"Certainly. Stuart is being helped with his breathing, so please don't be alarmed. George has had an operation on his broken limbs so he is still sleeping. Neither will be able to communicate with you today. I suggest you see them, talk to them (although they won't be able to answer) and then come back tomorrow."

He stood up and led my parents to the respective wards. First to George, who looked peaceful and then to Stuart. Their younger son was unconscious; his breathing was being assisted by machines surrounding his bed. An air of sadness hung between them and their child. I think Dad guessed at this point that they were going to lose him, but did not voice this possibility to his wife.

They stayed at Stuart's bedside overnight, watching and praying for his recovery, but it was not to be. Three days later, my parents had to make the decision to allow the machines to be turned off and on the fourth morning, in the early hours, Stuart breathed his last earthly breath and was taken to be with God's young angels.

Death of a child must be devastating. When it is your brother, it is bad enough, but to be predeceased by your off-spring, who has so much of life in front of him, seems unfair and inexplicable.

Mother was like a zombie, almost on auto-pilot. Aunty Jane had come to stay with us and had brought our cousins, Mary and Timothy, which was a great help. Our Aunt took over the running of the house and we cousins played together after school. As Mary was twelve, she went to school with Lizzie and Timothy went into the top class at the village school. I was going there in September, so I was curious to know what he thought about it. I stayed most of the day with Mum, who cuddled me closely when she was awake, but when Aunty Jane went to the shops in the village she took me with her. I did not really understand about Stuart's death but Lizzie answered my questions and assured me that he was with Jesus in heaven as one of his angels. George was making good progress in hospital, but would not be allowed home for some time.

At first, Mum and Dad had to use Jim's Taxis for everything, as Dad did not have the luxury of thinking if he should 'empty the ashtray, or buy a new car' as is often the case. A car was essential and he soon managed to find another Humber to replace the smashed up Snipe. Initially, Dad appeared to be philosophical about the situation that had presented itself in our life, but that was probably because he knew that someone must remain strong. Our poor mother became more snappy, more tired, more tearful. Thank goodness Aunty Jane was there. I don't think we would have eaten if it had been left to Mum. Stuart's funeral was about nine days after the crash.

Lizzie stayed at home with us. She had been devastated that her little brother had died at such a tender age.

"Unfortunately, he would do anything that George suggested so it isn't surprising that this has happened," she announced to our cousins.

"It wasn't George's fault," said Timothy who was in awe of his elder cousin.

"He was driving," was the reply.

Poor Lizzie. How was she going to cope? She had learned to tread warily with her big brother and had taught me how to avoid too much conflict with him. Now, she was blaming him for the loss of her favourite, Stuart.

CHAPTER 17

AFTERMATH

In a village, the church can be the lynch pin of the community. Our vicar was a remarkable man. The spirit worked through him. He oozed kindness, care, consideration for others and a love of Jesus. His sermons were more like talks than homilies and he captured the imaginations of everyone, whatever age. Once he and his wife had settled they had started groups for women and men and continued to work hard for our benefit. A young couple in the congregation, who came to live in the village when they got married, had started a youth group which had gradually grown to fourteen members. It was a thriving church.

You entered the building at the door round the back from the main road. There was an old, iron gate which was closed when no services were in progress. The pathway after the three steps, was flanked by flowers and shrubs which led to grave stones on the left and the west side of the church on the right. As you turned the corner a substantial oak door led into a porch where walls were covered with notices; flower rotas, names of past vicars, wardens, keyholders with their addresses, information about the present incumbant and times of services. There was a special notice board about the groups that had been started, as they were held in the church hall which was down the main street, about five minutes walk from the church.

The church was built from that beautiful big grey stone from which so many 15th century churches are constructed. It had a feeling of perpetual fortitude, safety and peacefulness. The ancient flagged floor rang out as you trod on it and the red carpet which ran the length of the nave between rows of flanking pews, was threadbare and faded. It was homely. There were some new hassocks littered along the pews in between the more grubby older ones. The women's groups were running a project which entailed making replacement hassocks over the year. The theme was ' our village' and some interesting designs had already emerged; the Green, the duckpond, the church, the church hall and the stalls at the summer fete including 'smack Fred!' Mother was naturally now intent on making one in memory of our brother Stuart.

Within all congregations, there is always one person (often a 'bossy woman') who tries to control everything. There is no disputing that Maisie Groom worked hard for the church but she was bossy, inquisitive, outspoken and a gossip. However, if anyone said anything to her that she did not like, approve of or agree with, she became vindictive and belligerent. Not a great model of Christianity! Of course, most people treated her carefully, with far more respect than she deserved, and smiled when she spoke with them, holding their own counsel.

At this sad time, my mother did not have the patience that she had previously shown with Maisie. When she informed Mother what flowers would be put into the church for Stuart's funeral the retort was, " There will be spring flowers. Stuart is too little to have the usual lilies."

"That's not what they should be," started Maisie.

"That's what they will be," replied Mother, "and my sister and I will be arranging them."

"You shouldn't," replied Maisie.

"He was my child, Maisie and I shall do what I like without any interference from you."

It is reported that people held their breathes at this retort from Mother, as Maisie was led away by one of her more sensible hench-women who said quietly, " Beryl is very distressed at the moment. I think it's best to just let this happen. Eh?"

Of course most people also knew that you didn't push Beryl Harper too far either. Needless to say, Mother and Aunty Jane supplied the spring flowers for the church. On the Sunday after the funeral Lizzie pointed them out to me. Tiny posies sat in vases on the window ledges and two displays stood in the nave and at the chancel steps where they must have guarded Stuart's coffin during the service before it was taken to the graveyard in the grounds. We went to look at the small mound which was also covered with spring flowers after the service.

Eventually, a stone was erected which read:

'Our dear son Stuart
(Dec.1942-April 1955)
At rest with Jesus.'

It is funny how people choose to sit in the same pew every Sunday. Our family usually occupied the fourth pew back on the south side of the church. The preacher could use the pulpit on the north side although our vicar often chose to stand on the chancel steps. The choir stalls and organ were behind him filled with the usual singers. Mr Brooks, another pharmacist who worked in Bristol was the organist. He was a big burly man with a heart of gold and a sense of humour which matched his large frame. He held the respect of the three basses and two tenors whilst charming the five sopranos and three altos. The five remaining boys (now that Stuart had died) were in serious awe of their choir master and he had created a joyous atmosphere amongst his followers. When it was the summer fete, the choir took responsibility for erecting the tables and providing seating which was a very important activity. Naturally, some members were occupied with other aspects of the church as it was policy to involve as many people as possible.

The altar at the east end of the church was shrouded in a white cloth and the frontal was in the correct liturgical colour. There was a simple cross to remind us that Jesus died for our sins but rose again to promise us eternal life with our father in heaven. We needed this reminder frequently after Stuart died and I always felt he was with us when we were in church, although it was hard to see the choir boys in their places without him. George had long abandoned singing in the choir although Dad insisted that we attended church as a family.

The east widow was very old. The muted colours added reverence and serenity to that special area of the building. Creation was cleverly depicted around the main glass which was dominated by the life of Jesus. As our church was dedicated to Saint James, although he was probably not present at the crucifixion, he appeared at the foot of the cross in our east window. Lizzie taught me to recognise him by looking for the shell that he always holds. I later learned that the shell is a symbol associated with one of the legends which grew up after his death. The disciples of Jesus wanted to return him to Santiago de Compostela in Spain. There was a storm, the body was lost overboard and it was washed ashore covered with shells. Do all Apostles have legends associated with them? Were the early church members anxious to make them memorable? Was it not sufficient that they lived with our Lord during his earthly sojourn? Oh, the wonders of religion! Whatever you believe, our church was a place of God and duly loved by its members, who were protective of all - even Maisie - if any outsider offered any criticism.

When it was time for the sermon in the morning service, the children were ushered out into the porch and shepherded down the path to the Church Hall. I truly loved my Sunday school teacher, whose name was Joan. She was a 'buxom lass' (Dad's phrase) who had a round face, with soft skin and a heavenly smile. At seventeen, she was a trainee hairdresser and her own dark hair was cut in a bob, haloing her lovely face and making her features quite angelic. She told us Bible stories with such vivacity and described the situation so vividly, that I thought I was actually in Palestine. Her lessons on Elijah and Elisha were so inspiring that I can remember them to this day. In retrospect, I think she opened my mind to the works and words of the Prophets.

However, Joan was on the receiving end of Maisie's vicious tongue. She tried to complain that Joan had 'favourites'. Evidently, these did not include Maisie's grandchildren, whom she felt missed the opportunity to answer questions or share their drawings and writings at the end of a lesson. Joan was either too holy to retaliate, or had learned to tread on egg shells so that Maisie did not cause any more trouble than was necessary. However, criticism, when you are just seventeen, presumably makes you question if it is worth surrendering two or three hours a week to teach small children. Within three months of the second incident, we youngest members of the church were deprived of the stories and smiles of our enthusiastic teacher. Although she continued to attend church she could not be persuaded to return to her teaching duties. Mother had to fill in the gap until a new teacher could be found. Somehow, Sunday school was not as exciting with her at the helm!

CHAPTER 18

CHANGES

Death can affect different people in different ways. Is it easier to see the loved one deteriorate gradually before your eyes, becoming prepared for the end? Or is the sudden taking better, knowing that the loved one was happy and healthy until the very last moment? For those left behind, the latter way is a bitter blow-well below the belt, leaving the body crumpled and the brain confused with jumbled frightening thoughts. Some are able to shed tears from the first moment of shock, others find the hurt numbing until the tears overflow some months later. Torrents, caused by a casual remark, a memory, an advert, a tune, a phrase, embarrass the shedder of the plump determined tears cascading down the cheeks of a distorted face, causing distress to the observer.

Our mother sobbed from the time that she knew of her boy's accident. When Stuart died she was the one that crumpled. She changed. And she gradually became more tolerant and forgiving of our misdemeanours! When I spilt my milk all over my dress, instead of the usual " be more careful" or "don't be so sloppy," my mother said, "Oh dear. Never mind." She promptly fetched a cloth to mop up the mess. One day George cut his trousers when he was 'carving' a piece of wood. At one time Mother would have admonished him and probably stopped his pocket money to pay for the repair. On this occasion she was conciliatory saying, " Don't worry. We can easily mend the slash in the material." In fact, Father remarked that she was getting soft in her old age. She only smiled and said, " Life's too short to be cross all the time."

I am sure that people in the village noticed her change of personality but we would have been the last people to hear their views. She often mentioned Stuart. Sometimes she spoke of him in the present tense as if he was still alive. When Lizzie pointed this out to her she replied, "But my darling Lizzie, he is still alive in my heart. He is here with us in spirit even if his body has gone. I have four children to love and four children who love Dad and me."

Dad, however, became quieter than ever. He did not want to talk about his younger son. He chose to work alone in the garden when he came home from his day job. He found solace with his chickens in their hen house. Whilst George was recovering in hospital Lizzie became even more motherly towards me. She would often take me by the hand and we would go in search of our Father to see if we could help or to ensure that he was not lonely. Lizzie and I talked about Stuart; I wanted to know what had happened to him now that he had died. Lizzie explained that God still needed him in heaven to be an angel for him, so that he could look after us and make life on earth easier for us. She explained about guardian angels, said that we could still talk to Stuart, feel him with us, be glad that he had been happy and had never suffered. In later life she told me that talking to me about Stuart had helped her to grieve, come to terms with his passing, forgive George and realize that his death was an accident.

Our parents were very proud of our achievements. Certificates were framed and hung on walls alongside the 'cries of London' and the ugly brass plates that Mother favoured. There was a lovely photograph of we four children taken at a professional photographers which hung in the hall. After Stuart's death it was moved on to the wall in the sitting room, 'so that we can all be together in the evenings' explained our Mother. (My desire to surround myself with photographs of loved ones must have come from her!)

Bob, probably recalling his moments of freedom, moped around the kitchen sniffing the legs of the chair that Stuart always sat on at the table. Our beautiful dog only sprang into life when Lizzie and Dad suggested 'walkies'. He liked it best when the whole family accompanied him on these expeditions. Once he was released from his lead he could bound over the fields, sniff out the smell of rabbits, chase imaginary ones, bark and forget his worries. The fresh air and the natural world was the best antidote to the sorrow of death. As a depleted family, we would return invigorated from Bob's 'walkies' ready to face the world again.

Mum and Dad were able to visit George in his hospital bed with renewed compassion eager to ensure that their elder son didn't feel himself to blame for the death of his little brother. Lizzie's gentle disposition was refueled so that her patience with me whenever our parents were out knew no bounds. She and I read books, completed jigsaws on the large dining room table, listened to the few gramophone records that the family owned and sang and talked endlessly until it was time for me to get ready for bed. A big sister is a joy and I thought that everybody should have one. She and my imaginary friends eased the heartache and the moments of loneliness. Ruby had developed arthritis and so was unable to go for walks, so I often wondered if Bob had an imaginary friend to run with when he went out. With her wise words and actions, Lizzie eased the transition from being one of four children to being the youngest of three. Although I was the adopted child, I was never made to feel that I did not belong in this family. I always felt cherished.

The person who changed more than anyone else in our family was George. He was in hospital for six weeks after the crash and so was unable to attend the funeral of his brother. The vicar spent special hours with him convincing George that he was not to blame for our brother's untimely death. I am sure that he also urged him to be more considerate, thoughtful and aware of the consequences of his actions now that he was the only son left in the house. I certainly found him less bullish and domineering when he returned home. Sometimes he was almost gentle and loving. Although he was studying for 'A' levels he made time for me and sometimes read me a story or placed me on his knee. He spoke to both Lizzie and me with more love than he had previously shown; he seemed to be trying to compensate for the last years. He and Lizzie became better friends than they had once been and George was more respectful of her. She seemed to understand that he needed her support and love. Although she had initially blamed him she was sensible and realized that he had not killed Stuart deliberately. Eighteen months after the crash, George went to university in London, where he met Belinda whom he later married. They were very happy, especially when their children were born. The two boys had their father's good looks and the lovely disposition of their mother. George and Belinda spent quality hours with them moulding them into delightful children.

Perhaps Stuart's death had not been entirely in vain.

Despite the outside show of recovery and normality I am sure we all missed Stuart's presence. I missed his laugh, his nudges, his smile, his sense of fun, his encouragement, his gentle persuasiveness, his being. I held memories of almost five years, what a bucketful must have been in Lizzie's and George's minds. As for our parents...

CHAPTER 19

DOUBLE AGENT

Robert Halford heard of the tragedy that had befallen the Harper family when he went to the local shop on the Tuesday morning following the accident. He decided to act in a neighbourly way and write a note of condolence, which he slipped through the letter box on Wednesday.

He found a seat at the back of the church for the funeral service and decided that he could call on the family within the week. By Saturday, he had made the decision to attend the church service on Sunday; that would make him a true member of the village community. He managed to shake Mr Harper's hand at the back of the church but Mrs Harper was surrounded by members of the congregation paying their respects.

As Robert looked out of his window on the following Wednesday afternoon he saw Mrs Harper pegging out clothes on her washing line. She had the little girl in tow. Why wasn't she at school? Perhaps she was poorly? Deciding to satisfy his curiosity he went and knocked on their door.

"Hello Mrs Harper," he said, turning on his charm, " I hope that I find you a little better."

"Yes thank you Mr Halford."

"Is your little girl not feeling very well?"

"Oh no. She doesn't go to school yet. Not until September. The other children are out at school so the house feels quiet and lonely at the moment." Tears welled in her eyes and Robert instinctively touched his neighbour's hand.

"Oh...I'm going in to have a cup of tea. Would you like to join me?"

"Well thank you dear lady."

What an opportunity had presented itself to learn more about this family and the little girl, who grabbed his hand and pulled him over the doorstep.

Beryl made a pot of tea and poured a glass of milk for Judith. She took the cake tin out of the pantry. Fortunately, Jane had left the family well stocked up with fruit cake. Beryl realized that she must start getting herself organised so that her family could get back to normal; or as normal as was possible in the circumstances.

"May I offer you a slice of cake?" she asked solicitously.

"Thank you Mrs Harper."

"Oh please call me Beryl."

" O.K. I'm Robert."

Robert took a bite of the Dundee cake which had been given to him. "Umm. Delicious."

"It's my sister's handiwork today, not mine. I'm afraid I've not got round to chores until now."

Her eyes filled with tears again and I climbed onto her knee as she sank onto one of the kitchen chairs.

"I'm so so sorry," Robert Halford said gently.

"Thank you. Please don't be sympathetic or I'll dissolve again," Beryl urged with a smile while at the same time hugging me closer to her.

"No. Let's be more practical. Why not tell me something about yourself."

With that my mother opened up her heart. She told Robert everything about us: Dad's foibles, George's headstrong ways, although she shared these gently remembering that he was still recovering in hospital, Lizzie's gentleness, Stuart's charm and then, smiling down at me, the joy that I had brought to the family when I had arrived five years ago. Mum then invited Robert to talk about himself. In retrospect, I suspect that most of what he said was untrue. We shall never know if he had a wife, two children, a house or holiday home, as we 'learned' at the kitchen table on that day in April 1955.

We were still sitting at the table when Lizzie came through the door.

"Goodness. Is it that time already?"

"Don't worry Mum. Angie's mother gave me a lift home. Hello my treasure," she added smiling at me. "What have you been up to?"

"I must go," stated Robert rising from his chair. "Thank you for the tea, the cake and the chat. See you soon."

"Lizzie, could you show Mr Harper out?" said our Mother, smiling at our neighbour. "Goodbye Robert. Come on Judith. We'd better get some tea on the table before Daddy gets home."

"Are you and Dad going to see George tonight?" asked Lizzie coming back into the kitchen.

"Well Yes. I expect so."

"Could I go one evening?" asked Lizzie.

"Of course dear. Perhaps you'd like to go instead of me?"

"Not really Mum. You should go. But Angie's mum has offered to baby-sit Judith one evening if that's O.K."

"We'll see," said Mum. " I'll talk to Dad about it," she said, smiling tenderly at us both. "Now let's get on with our jobs. Go and change, Lizzie, whilst Judith and I get started on the vegetables. It's a good job that it's chops tonight. I can just pop them in the Aga and let it do its work so that everything can be ready when Daddy gets home!" she said as she tied up my poppy patterned pinny.

When Lizzie returned dressed in her 'everyday dress' she put on her apron. It was a bought one and made of the usual plain material: not like mine, which had been made by Mummy, from an old summer dress. I did not appreciate how talented Mum was when I was small. In fact, in the 1950s and 60s most of the mothers I knew were able to cook, sew and clean in order to keep their homes spruce and their families healthy and well turned out with limited finances.

"What did Mr Harper want?" asked Lizzie inquisitively. She wasn't sure what to make of this man who was infiltrating her family.

"I'm not sure," replied our mother. " I think he was just being neighbourly."

"He was in church as well on Sunday."

"Yes. Your father said that he came and had a word with him after the service. Betty Lord said he was at Stuart's funeral."

"I saw him," I piped up.

"Ah good," replied our mother. "Now let's get started."

My mother was very tied up with her tasks and deep in thought.

Robert often knocked on the door after that and was usually invited in by Mother to have a cuppa. She felt a need to chat, especially about Stuart. Mr Halford, knowing nothing about our circumstances, made a ready audience. Temporarily, she forgot that he had asked so many questions in the village shop which had made her confide in her sister about the new neighbour. She also ignored the fact that Jane had come over on the bus to console her when she was panicking. Or that she had initially felt threatened by the man's strange interest in her youngest daughter. A listening ear is very comforting in time of sorrow. Beryl began to look forward to her neighbour's visits and the opportunity it gave her to unburden. Stanley was very supportive, but he was at work and she needed someone to talk to during the day. Anyway, Stanley had become so tired and introverted and happy to spend hours on his own. Hospital visiting took up many evenings. Beryl was lonely. Robert had become more than a neighbour, a friend. All seemed well- on the surface.

CHAPTER 20

SUSPICIONS

Birthdays are usually exciting times. We had all rallied round each other on our special days but after Stuart's death they were difficult occasions. He had only been dead for a matter of weeks before my fifth birthday so I wasn't able to have the elaborate celebrations that were customary in our family. Mum's birthday was a few days later and she hardly managed a smile, although Lizzie had insisted that the cards still had pride of place on the mantlepiece whilst mine were demoted to the window ledge. Lizzie was fifteen at the end of June and, as it was a school day, she brought her friend Angela home for a cup of tea and a slice of cake. It was all very low key and tinged with sadness, especially as George was still in hospital for my birthday. He was released on June 1st the day before Mum's birthday and Dad had the morning off work to collect him. He looked older, more serious and ashen faced.

"You'll soon be better with home cooking and fresh air," said Mum welcoming him back into the coop. She fussed around him until he told her, roughly in my opinion, that he was all right. He was on crutches, but insisted that he would be able to return to school before the end of term.

" I need to be there and get work for the holidays. I have got to do well; to get to university. I'm going to be a doctor."

"Oh. Yes dear. That will be a rewarding career."

"They do such wonderful things. I must repay their work and I'm going to do it for Stu's sake."

Mother's eyes filled with tears and she put her arms round her eldest child saying, " That's a great idea George. Well done!"

Lizzie beamed when Mum recounted the event to her upon her return from school. George had his leg up in the sitting room and was resting, which meant that he had actually fallen asleep and was snoring loudly. He made a steady recovery and with our parents and the vicar's help began to feel more at ease with the fact that he had been driving the car when Stuart met his death. Sometimes, Lizzie had been allowed to visit him while he was in hospital and Angela's mother came to our house to babysit me. As I was in bed before she arrived I rarely saw her and whether she looked in on me I have no idea. Once Teddy and I had cuddled down I seemed unable to stay awake, despite my firm intentions to ask Lizzie how our big brother was progressing. Had it been Lizzie in hospital there may have been more of an incentive to hear the verdict; but George had been very mean to me and I had not yet learned about forgiveness or turning the other cheek so I had less interest in him. I felt that it was his fault that Stuart was dead. I found it difficult to understand why everyone else was anxious to lift that burden from him. He was a pig-headed bully who had manipulated his younger brother at every possible opportunity, encouraged his adulation and made him idolise him, the elder boy. I don't expect that I rationalised my feelings into words when I was just five but I felt very cross with George for messing up our happy lives and spoiling our birthdays. He had become the centre of our existence, causing our parents to age and tire from daily visiting and although he was getting better, the hole caused by the loss of Stuart seemed to be growing deeper and wider. It was so unfair.

Three months after Stuart's death the weather was perfect. A true summer's day with a blue sky and a big yellow ball piercing the azure and spreading warmth into everyone's body and disposition. Beryl Harper was beginning to feel more sanguine about life without her younger son, Lizzie and George were making the most of their years at school whilst I tried to be a good girl, entertained myself and anticipated 'proper schooling' in September.

Stanley was finding that the loss of Stuart had given him a heavy heart and much to his own amazement a desire to be alone with his thoughts once his working day was finished. He often wondered if it was because he had showered his affection and empathy on to his wife, staying a tower of strength for her, that he had forgotten his own need to mourn properly. Now he felt numb and loveless. He found excuses to be out in the garden or in his shed and even opted out of bedtime stories. Beryl became worried about this change in her husband and when Robert visited, inadvertently blurted out her concerns. He was delighted to be able to offer a listening ear and become a daily visitor to the house.

On her return from school one Thursday afternoon towards the end of the academic year in July, Lizzie found their mother and Mr Halford in the back garden, enjoying a cup of tea, a slice of cake and an obvious joke. Lizzie watched them through the kitchen window and decided that her mother's behaviour was coquettish and she was openly flirting with their neighbour. She was furious!

Storming out of the back door she demanded, "And what do you two think you're doing? Haven't you got a job of work Mr Halford? And shouldn't you, Mother, be preparing dinner for your husband and children?"

Beryl was stunned. Lizzie, her usually gentle daughter, showing antagonism was simply unheard. Anyway, how DARE she speak like this to an adult? She got out of her chair, took hold of her daughter's arm, turned her away from Mr Halford and spat, "Remember your manners my girl."

"Remember who you're married to. I've watched you flirting with each other."

"There's nothing wrong with sharing a cup of tea with a neighbour."

"Not the way you're doing it. You don't look as if you've recently lost a son or you're a middle aged woman with a husband and three children at home. You're acting like a tart."

"That's enough. Go indoors. I'll speak to you later."

"I think I'd better go Beryl. I'll see you some time next week," interrupted Robert. " Goodbye Lizzie. Don't get the wrong idea. It's not what you think."

"It isn't?" replied Lizzie. "You're up to something - I don't know what exactly - but it isn't nice, and neither are you!"

"Indoors now!" snapped Beryl at her daughter. "Goodbye Robert. I'll sort this out."

When George and I saw our mother grab Lizzie's arm we realized that our sister had done something really bad to annoy Mother. George decided he would be safer escaping to the front room until he could be helped to his bedroom and I continued my colouring at the kitchen table. Our mother's look of anxiety was only seen by our outspoken sister.

"Well?" asked the older woman.

"Well. What?" replied her recalcitrant daughter.

"Whatever were you thinking of? That was quite out of character for you."

"I was mad. Poor Daddy. He can't recover and we're all still so sad but you...you...you were so distraught at first and we rallied round and now you're flirting with Mr Halford, who I wouldn't trust in any circumstances. AND YOU'RE LAUGHING like a school girl. It's just not right," she finished running out of words and bursting into tears.

Beryl put her arms around her daughter and held her tightly to her. After a few minutes Lizzie was able to compose herself.

"Go and change and then come down for a drink and a piece of cake. We'll talk about the situation in a minute. Don't forget to wash your face."

Beryl filled the kettle and wondered if she had been flirting a little with Robert. Stanley had become very distant recently but perhaps she should be trying to help him break down the barrier he had erected rather than entertaining their neighbour. Perhaps she wasn't as loving or attentive as she had used to be in the past. It was only later that Beryl admitted that she had felt unnerved by Robert Halford and alarmed that she had shared so many confidences with a man she didn't know that well and who asked those worrying questions of Betty Lord in her shop.

CHAPTER 21

SUNDAY LUNCH

As a child I remember that the month of August was glorious. Sun streamed through the kitchen window of Number 14; it also shone on Number 16 and Number 12. The roses responded to its warmth and opened their buds to acknowledge it. Rabbits hopped around in the adjoining field and Bob lazed in the garden.

We prepared for church. Mother pottered in the kitchen. Lizzie cut up root vegetables, George scraped potatoes, Father tidied and then Lizzie helped me lay the table ready for our Sunday dinner. The leg of lamb was cooking in the Aga so that there would only be vegetables to add later. We set off to church for the morning service. Such summer days were heaven on earth. The shadows from trees and houses, seemed in retrospect, to foretell the shadow that was about to fall over our family life. The church service was peaceful and people in the congregation smiled comfortingly as they always did.

But, things were soon to change. On arrival home, we found that the Aga had cooked our Sunday meal of lamb, roast potatoes and roasted vegetables while we had been in church. Mother cooked a cabbage after returning from the service and Lizzie and I took Bob for a short walk. Heaviness hung in the air and a deep sorrow swamped our home. Our Father had inspected the garden in the lull between church and Sunday dinner. Lizzie had supervised me changing from best to everyday clothes and had herself donned a rather sophisticated grey dress with a lace collar, bought for the funeral, which she had refused to keep for best but had demoted to everyday wear. George was still struggling to climb up the stairs so he had been excused changing his clothes as no adult was available to assist him up the steep flight and help him and so he had been allowed to stay in the kitchen. He had put the finishing touches to the table by laying condiments of salt, pepper and mint sauce.

Mother called us to the table. Father had carved the meat onto our plates and the vegetables steamed from their dishes. During the week food was served directly on to plates and passed to us individually, but Sunday dinner was a special family time and an opportunity to learn how to use serving spoons, pour wayward gravy and make small talk; all in preparation for an awaiting wider world.

George's appetite had returned, Lizzie ate sparingly, Father, who usually enjoyed good home cooking, seemed reluctant to enter into the spirit of the banquet, I had forgotten the gnawing pains in my stomach and our poor Mother was unable to do justice to the delicious feast which she had prepared. Suddenly, her sob broke the silence at the table. It became a wail and we all dropped our cutlery and turned towards her. Our Father was by her side in an instant cradling her in his arms, Lizzie cuddled me as we both shed tears in sympathy and George stared straight ahead. Eventually, Mother composed herself sufficiently to say, " We musn't let this food go to waste. I'll be alright in a minute."

" O.K.," replied Dad, patting her hand and then retiring to his own chair, " but we all need to talk."

How we struggled through that meal I will never know and we all agreed mutually to abandon the apple pie and custard until we felt more like eating it.

" We'll clear the table and wash up later," announced Dad, collecting the plates and cutlery together. " Lizzie, bring those mats and condiments too."

" I'll make us a cuppa," said Mum, smiling wanly. " Would you like milk or milky tea?" she asked me.

"I'd like a tea please," I replied, realizing that I needed to be like the rest of the family for the talk that was to follow.

Father gathered us together and ushered us through into the sitting room whilst Mother made a pot of tea for her brood. We sat around in the sitting room like people who hardly knew each other; strangers. Had we had a large polished table in the middle, we could have been at a board meeting for some prestigious firm. It felt very formal. Mother brought in a tray and offered us our tea, then she sat down next to our Father on the old lumpy sofa that was usually associated with comfort for Lizzie and me when we were watching a television programme.

"Now," began Father in a business-like voice, "Let's see where this is going."

I looked enquiringly at my big sister who gave me a reassuring smile and willed me not to say anything.

"Beryl dear. Is there anything worrying you?"

"No," snapped Mother. "Just the death of Stuart."

We children held our breath. We now had need to tread very carefully on those eggshells. As Lizzie remarked to me afterwards, 'at least some of mother's spark had returned!'

"Shall I take Judith for a walk?" asked the naturally diplomatic Lizzie.

"Good idea love," replied Father.

Lizzie looked meaningfully at George.

"I ought to catch up with some school work," he said, easing himself out of the chair.

"I'll help you upstairs then," Dad offered. "Lizzie, get yourself and Judith organised and you, my darling," he said, tenderly touching his wife's hand, "hang on while I take George upstairs and I'll be back."

On his completion of that task Stanley came back to a still tearful Beryl.

"It's all come to a head," she started to explain. "And I've been talking a lot to Robert who has been a rock."

"Yes, we should all be grateful for his friendship," added Stanley.

"But..." Beryl paused.

"Yes?" asked her husband encouragingly.

"I'm still not sure about him though. He confuses me...I know he's a really nice man but he knows too much."

"What do you mean by that?"

"Well, he manipulates answers out of me."

"Oh?"

"Before I know what I've said he knows more than I really intended saying."

"Is there anything in particular that you don't like, that worries you?"

"Well, yes. When he first came I remember he asked lots of questions down in the shop about Judith. What with all that's happened I had forgotten about that but I was thinking the other night in bed, he wheedles things out of me and especially where she is concerned. I feel that he is asking too many questions-in the nicest way mind you."

"And Stuart?" reminded her husband.

"I don't think I'll ever lose this feeling of loss and helplessness. Let the children think that's the only thing I'm worrying about. They seem to like Robert and would be horrified that I thought his friendship might have an ulterior motive."

"Oh, I see. Do you want me to tackle him?"

"You know, I think I do."

"O.K. I'll ask if he'd like to meet; probably over a pint to ease the situation would be best..."

"That's a good idea. I'm sure he's after something."

"I'll ask him. O.K.?"

Beryl nodded, feeling a sense of relief.

"Do you feel a bit better now?" Stanley asked.

"Umm. Thank you, my darling. I fear I've been wrapped up too much in my own sorrow and not been much of a support for you. I'm sorry."

"Perhaps I should have been more open and not made myself into a bit of a recluse. Let's try and remember to grieve together and we'll get through this black cloud." He patted Beryl's knee. "Come on, we'd better try to reassure the other children; they're our priority now."

CHAPTER 22

THE HEN AND CHICKEN

Robert heard the letter box as he was shaving on Monday morning. He heard Stanley's car drive off to Bristol but he didn't connect the two events and so was slightly stunned to open the envelope that he found on the front door mat and draw out a letter from his neighbour. It suggested a meeting at the local pub, the 'Hen and Chicken' on Wednesday evening at 7.30 p.m. as there were some issues which he wished to discuss with him. Meanwhile, Stanley would appreciate it if he did not visit either Beryl or the children as it was now their summer holidays. He continued that they needed to get back to some kind of normality and as the children were now home for six weeks this would provide an ideal opportunity. Stanley hoped that they would be able to come to terms with their loss together. Should Robert be unable to meet him on the Wednesday, then could he let him know by a note through his letter box suggesting an alternative date and time.

Robert decided that he would happily meet up with his neighbour in the secret hope that he would be able to glean further information about Judith from her father's point of view. So he made sure that he was sitting in the 'Hen and Chicken' by 7.15 in a corner suitable for a private, neighbourly chat. Although Stanley bought the first round on his arrival, it was clear that his feathers were ruffled. Once in his seat, he was quick to get to the point.

"I thought you were a friend, Robert, but I expect there's a bit more to it?"

"Whatever are you getting at?"

"Well, you're either making a play for my wife, and the state she's in at the moment since the loss of Stuart makes her into a very vulnerable being, or there is something even more sinister going on in your mind."

Robert looked enquiringly at his neighbour.

"The number of questions you have been asking," continued Stanley, "isn't normal for a neighbour."

"I was only making conversation," protested Robert.

"Oh yes!" retorted Stanley. "Do you think I came up with the last bunch of recruits? So, why was Judith your main topic of conversation with Betty Lord, that time in her shop? Why did you 'wheedle' (which was the word used by Beryl by the way) information about our family out of everyone you came across?"

"That makes me sound like a manipulative bastard, which I am not."

"If the cap fits? ...Just what are you?" demanded Stanley. "You never seem to go out to work, I've hardly ever seen you in Bristol and from what I can make out from the children, you're often in my house! So, I suggest you come up with a good explanation before I have you investigated, Robert."

"Well, Stanley, you see." Robert prevaricated.

"Oh come on man. That approach isn't going to get us anywhere."

" O.K I'll come clean. I'm a Private Investigator."

A stunned Stanley was taken off guard.

"What? Whatever are you investigating?"

"Isn't it obvious?"

The penny dropped. "Oh no. Not our Judith?"

"Ummm. Someone wants to trace her."

"Her mother has signed all the papers for adoption. We're not going to give her back. She's ours," snapped Stanley.

"Of course she is," reassured Robert, " and her mother doesn't even want to know where she lives or anything about her."

"So, who does?"

"Her grandparents."

"Hm. And why is that?"

"Well, only the girl's mother knew of her daughter's pregnancy until recently, when she told her husband. She was present at the birth and was very troubled about her granddaughter being given up, but her daughter refused to be diverted from the path which she had chosen. My clients now want to make contact with the child."

"Well it won't be as grandparents. Judith already has them in her family."

"Perhaps they could be 'long lost friends' of Beryl's mother, who could be passing and drop in for tea...or something like that?" suggested Robert.

"I'll have to discuss it with my wife. I'll let you know what we think by letter. Meanwhile," added Stanley downing the remainder of his pint, " you are never, NEVER to cross my threshold again. I feel deeply betrayed by someone who I thought had become a family friend - only to discover that he was friendly in order to complete a job. Perhaps someone should have warned you that asking direct questions can only lead to suspicions. A competent P.I. would have known that a more circumspect investigation would make life easier for himself. Now," Stanley emphasised by rising from his seat, "you must excuse me and allow me to return to my family. I suggest you find another job and move away from here."

With this, Stanley turned on his heel and left the pub.

Robert bought himself another pint of bitter and considered his options. It was obviously time to move on, which was probably a good thing as he felt that his relationship with Beryl was progressing beyond friendship or business, and that could have led to problems and uncertainties. He would contact the landlord and terminate his lease. Once he'd heard from Stanley, he could write to Mr and Mrs Malvern with news of Judith and her family. Contented, he finished his pint and made his way home.

Two days after his meeting with Stanley, Robert opened another letter that fell on to his mat in the early morning.

"Dear Mr Halford,

I have discussed the situation with my wife. We have decided that you should ask your clients to pretend that they are old friends of my mother in law and ask them to write a letter so that we can share it with the children. If we like what we read, we can then arrange a date for them to come to tea. BUT, no reference is to be made about them being grandparents of Judith and nothing is to be said about their daughter in relation to her child. (I expect Lizzie will want to know if they have any children and what they do - she's not nosey, just an interested, kind girl who likes people.)

Trusting we shall never meet again.
Yours sincerely,
S.R. Harper"

"That's put me in my place," thought Robert, "but it's a good result for the Malverns - and I'll be able to invoice them with my accompanying letter."

Robert knew that with this fee, he would be able to enjoy a holiday in his favourite hotel in Sidmouth before embarking on another lucrative investigation. Being single suited his choice of career and as his own man he was able to do just as he pleased, when he pleased. Anyway, there was a pleasant little lady in Sidmouth who enjoyed his charming company; once he had written the necessary letter to the Malverns he could organise his trip and drop her a line too.

Robert Halford was not the sort of person who would remain thwarted for long.

CHAPTER 23

A TEA PARTY

The letter from Bernard and Stella Morgan duly arrived asking the Harpers if they could drop by for tea when they were returning from holiday at the beginning of September. They asked about the children's ages so that they could bring them small presents, as befitted people who had never met them before, but knew of them from contact with their grandmother.

September 3rd arrived and Beryl set the table in the dining room for the occasion. She had made delicate cucumber sandwiches, corned beef and egg sandwiches (for her hungry children), fruit cake and a Victoria sponge. I, who was due to start school at the end of the next week, insisted on making my speciality (Rice-Krispy cakes) because " everybody likes them, Mummy."

When the Malverns arrived in their Jaguar Beryl's heart missed a beat. They were obviously wealthy business people and she immediately felt out of her depth.

"Don't worry," reassured Stanley as he noticed his wife's stricken expression, "they'll be polite and eager to please. We have the commodity that they would like."

The doorbell sprang to life and Stanley made his way from the sitting room into the hall. It had been arranged for the children and his wife to stay in that room when they heard the bell so that they were all in place ready to be introduced when Stanley returned. Beryl could see that Stella Malvern, a petite lady of 54, wore fashionable clothes as would befit a middle-class person living in London. Her husband wore the air of a business man. He looked ill-at-ease in casual clothes and he sported a tie despite the warmth of the day. However, they were extremely 'agreeable'(as the French would say)and had kindly brought presents of books suitable for the children's ages. Beryl had received the bouquet of flowers that Bernard had presented her with when he came into the sitting room and hurried to the kitchen to put them into a vase of water. Whilst there, she filled the kettle to make a pot of tea and removed the covers from the sandwiches and cakes which she placed on the dining room table. She then returned to the sitting room to find Stella in conversation with the girls and Stanley entertaining Bernard whilst her eldest child stood attentively nearby.

"Excuse me," she said as she entered, "you may like to use the bathroom after your journey before we have tea. Lizzie, would you kindly show Mr and Mrs Malvern where it is and then we shall all prepare ourselves for tea. Judith, come into the kitchen and we can wash our hands and make a pot of tea. Can you organise George, darling?" she asked of her husband.

Soon, they were all seated in front of a veritable feast and Beryl was pouring tea for the imposters before her. Lizzie asked how long they had known her grandma. Stella explained that she had been a friend of her neighbour and they had met when Beryl's mother had visited once ' many years ago.'

"We got on really well so we exchanged addresses so that we could send Christmas cards."

"Oh, that was nice. I think we do things like that don't we Mum?"

"Oh yes," replied Beryl.

"Did you see my mother often? I expect you heard that she died a couple of years ago," added Beryl turning to look at Stella Malvern.

"Oh, of course, dear. Marge, our neighbour, told us so that we wouldn't send a card that Christmas; no need to cause unnecessary upset, is there? We were so sorry to hear of your sad loss. We only got your address when we told Marge where we were holidaying this year, so I couldn't send a sympathy letter. Anyway, I hope that it isn't an imposition to call in."

"Not at all," insisted Stanley. "We're glad to see you."

Beryl was not as sure as her husband. She was 'treading on eggshells.' This couple were NOT going to take me from her.

Once tea was completed and complements given to the cooks (I was delighted that Mr and Mrs Malvern had both eaten one of my Rice Krispy cakes) we children were dismissed to the sitting room. Bernard and Stanley were advised to chat whilst Stella offered her services in the kitchen to help Beryl with the washing up.

"Now we have made contact, we must meet again when it is convenient," suggested Stella.

"We'll have to see," replied a reluctant Beryl.

"May I send birthday cards and presents-for your mother's sake?"

"Well you could, but I'd be more comfortable if we moved away from that idea if you don't mind. It was a good way in for the children's sake, but I'd rather that they didn't muddle Mother's life up with yours."

"Oh. I have a photo of Judith's mother if you would like to have it for her."

"No, not at this point. Thank you. I really can't cope with her belonging to someone else. Once Judith is 21 she can obviously make up her own mind, but at present she's mine."

Stella nodded. "I'll make a scrap-book of the life of Judith's mother so that she can have it when she comes of age. Does she know that she was adopted?"

"Of course. She knows that we chose her because her mummy couldn't look after her and we could offer her a nice home with brothers and a sister. As she was only six weeks old when we had her, I feel as though she's always been mine! 'Adoption is when a child grows in her Mummy's heart instead of her tummy', as somebody once said."

"I'm sure dear. But can you try to understand how I feel? I was devastated that Elizabeth didn't want to keep her. There hasn't been a day when I haven't thought of the precious little bundle that I saw in Whipps Cross Hospital."

"What did your husband think?"

"Oh, he didn't know anything at the time."

"Really?" Beryl asked incredulously.

"He wouldn't have understood. Elizabeth often decided to travel so he didn't think anything of it when months went by without him seeing her."

"Right, but he must know now."

"Oh yes. He responded far better than either of us hoped."

Stella breathed deeply. "And Judith's mother? How is she?"

"Oh, she's furious. She has no desire to ever see her child again. We have to 'tread on eggshells' over this whole venture. She respects the position that when she signed the adoption papers to say she would make no contact with the child she meant it."

Beryl relaxed a bit at this. At least the mother wouldn't be worrying them. She felt sure that Stanley could handle the grandparents if necessary.

Stella continued, "It's been really good to meet you and know that Judith is being so well cared for here. She's obviously very happy."

"Oh yes. She loves her big sister and Lizzie is so good with her as you can see. Now she's about to start school. She's really a member of this village and belongs here now."

"Of course. We aren't going to bother you too much. Just wanted to know how the little girl was faring." Stella smiled and couldn't stop herself touching Beryl lightly on the arm. "Don't worry. We won't invade your life. I believe the Private Investigator is moving on shortly. He told my husband that his work was done and it was time to start another job."

"He's certainly an expert at wheedling his way into people's lives," Beryl said, with a hint of bitterness.

"I'm so sorry if it was too big an ordeal for you."

"No. Not now. But, we did feel hurt when we heard the truth at first, because we thought he had become a friend and therefore we probably gave him too much information about ourselves. It felt like a betrayal."

"Oh my dear, I do hope not. I expect he was trying to get more information for us."

"Yes. I expect that was so. Anyway, it's water under the bridge. Thank you for helping dry up. I'm glad that we've had the opportunity to chat."

After polite banter, Bernard suggested that it was time that he and his wife went home and "Left these dear people in peace." We children were summoned to say goodbye and once they had left Lizzie took me into the sitting room to watch the television and George suddenly remembered that he had homework to finish.

Beryl and Stanley discussed the visit and decided that they must keep this new contact at arm's length. From their conversations both had gleaned the feeling that it would not be too inclusive and that they would be able to carry on their lives as normal. We children did not discuss the visit and just accepted that these new people were part of our late grandma's life and therefore deserved some consideration and thoughtfulness. We were far more disturbed by Robert's departure as we had generally enjoyed his company and his jokes. He was relaxed and interesting as well as appearing kind. Lizzie was the only one who had been suspicious of him and even she could hardly believe that he was an Investigator, employed by somebody to find out details about her sister, Judith. How good it is to be young and accepting! Or, is it just the start of a steep learning curve?

CHAPTER 24

LEAVING THE COOP.

In the September after the crash, I was sent to school.

Lizzie and George went back to their school bus routine and life returned to as much normality as possible without Stuart. Father became less of a recluse, was more attentive to our Mother and to us as a family. Mother was less manic, resuming her sewing with Mrs. Holmes making garments for the African Missions. She and Aunty Jane seemed to meet more frequently, which was good for them both, although we rarely seemed to see our Uncle and cousins. (I suppose life was busy and it was difficult to travel anywhere without your own means of transport.) If Father needed our car, Mother could not commandeer it for visiting purposes. We were, after all, lucky to have the luxury of our own car; many people in the village had to rely on buses or the local man who ran the Taxi Service - when he was not delivering bread to the community.

Lizzie and George were both beginning the second year of examination courses, so they had lots of studying in the evenings, although they always made time to be with me. I feel so lucky to have had such caring, special people around me; even if my older brother had deprived me of my favourite one.

How do people remember the intricate details of their first encounter with school? I can remember very little of the actual day, and it is only with hearsay that I have any true recollections of the auspicious hours.

The only thing I was conscious of was the excitement and knowing that I would be like the rest of the family. We were used to Mum piling us into the car, so I was not at all alarmed at the event on the 9th of September, 1955. There were no 'rising fives' in those days and I was ready to be in a class with children of my own age. We had not really mixed with many children other than cousins, as my parent's 'friends' children were over twelve, so I was oblivious to peer pressure. There were no Nursery classes or Play Groups so that young mothers could enjoy a 'break' from the small children; just pure motherhood from dawn to dusk, something about which our Mother never complained. She often said that those days were the most fulfilling of her life.

She clung to me as she dropped me off with my new teacher and told me to be careful during the morning and that she would fetch me home for my midday meal and then bring me back for the afternoon schooling. In retrospect, I expect she was feeling anxious about leaving me - she had lost one child that year and had no intention of losing any others.

I fortunately knew some of the other children from Sunday School and general village life, so it was not too traumatic. The teacher was Mrs. Gale, who lived in the village so everyone already knew her, and she was kind but firm so it was easy to settle into the routine that she provided within the four walls of the classroom. We had indoor and outdoor shoes (so woe betide anyone who was not in the correct footwear at the correct time), and had to line up to go in and out of the building, or to leave the classroom at any time. There was to be no shouting out and one had to raise one's arm for everything, it seemed. At first we had Arithmetic before break, when we drank the most revoltingly sweet, warm milk and ate the snack that we had brought from home (a biscuit, or the like) and then we were allowed to play. After break and before lunch, we did Writing which consisted of English language exercises, our own compositions and the occasional poem. I usually skipped along by the side of my mother when she collected me at 12o'clock and then again when she returned me to school at 1.15pm. The afternoon session was different every day; Monday was History, Tuesday was Geography, Wednesday was Scripture, on Thursday afternoon we had Nature Study and Friday afternoon heralded Art. Every afternoon ended with a story, which settled us for home.

Gradually, as the days passed, I was allowed to stay to school dinners, which were taken in the basement of the school house called The Refectory. In retrospect I think it must have been a small private school; probably owned by an unqualified teacher who had enough money to buy a big enough house to convert three rooms into classrooms and a basement into a refectory.

I was happy at this school and my greatest memory was that a 'slow' boy was placed next to me so that I could help him with things he found difficult. I won countless stars and prizes - can I remember this or is it because I occasionally still come across an Enid Blyton book which says:

'Awarded to Judith Harper for coming top in stars.'

Two years later I had to leave that school and move to the Church of England School in the next village, Shalford. I made good progress and by the time I was eleven I had passed the scholarship, for which I was given a bike as a reward.

Both George and Lizzie had left to go to university. George read sciences, met his wife, Belinda and then trained to become a doctor. Lizzie read English at Birmingham and gained first class honours, to nobody's great surprise. She thought about a career in journalism, but Father pointed out that this was a world far too cut and thrust for her gentle temperament, so she became a teacher in a Girls' Grammar School in Bristol. When she married Thomas, who was a talented artist but whose day job was as a teacher at the Cathedral School, our mother was delighted. I was a bridesmaid at the wedding and wore a pretty 'ballerina' length white tulle dress which had pink rose buds on the top layer of net and a wide pink cummerbund around the middle. The outfit was completed with an 'alice-band' of pink rosebuds on white net, white socks and sandals and a posy of pink rose buds. I thought that I looked a Bobby-dazzler. I was twelve years old, had been cosseted all my life and was certainly not 'streetwise' as they say nowadays.

Like my birth grandfather I found that life doesn't get easier as you get older and that 'eggshells' did not become either less brittle or less copious. It took me many years to cope with the reactions of others to my quick tongue! Lizzie had been better trained as she grew up aware of George and Mother but she had always protected me and so was more alarmed by the cracking of shells when I scrambled a yolk.

I was expected to 'fulfill my potential' at Grammar School, but as everyone omitted to tell me what this was, I am still unsure as to whether I fulfilled it or failed to meet the criteria.

It was great fun to go on the bus with my friends, some of whom remain friends to this day - but there were blips along the route to adulthood. The staff were authoritarian and many appeared to be bitter and twisted. We all put this down to them being unmarried and childless. My mother was annoyed when I expressed these views and told me that some had probably lost loved ones during the war and that to judge them in such a way was both callous and thoughtless. Secretly, we thought that some of the 'old dragons' were heartless and had read too many books by Dickens. However, we did learn how to behave and that sometimes it is wiser to keep ones own counsel than to say what is truly on one's mind; I found this really difficult (and still do!) and had to learn the hard way!

We had a music teacher, Miss Smith, who had difficulty keeping discipline. We sat on forms in a non-specialist room and one Thursday we arranged to take it in turns to start a discussion with the girl in front when we were singing a song. Miss Smith had reprimanded three girls before it was my turn to be disruptive. Suddenly, she saw red. She screamed at me, gave me two order marks (three meant a trip to the Head Mistress' office in The Ivory Tower) and told me to report to her in the Music Room at break. Obviously, the prank was abandoned for that lesson and I shook for its remainder.

I made my way along to the place which would always be associated with my retribution. Sitting alongside Miss Smith was my form tutor. The latter told me that she was disappointed in me and that I was to choose my friends more carefully. I was also informed that my parents would be receiving a letter about my behaviour and that I should consider how badly I had let down the lovely people who had accepted me into their family. I was devastated and felt a deep resentment towards them for using the fact that I had been adopted as a lever to the discipline process. Fortunately, my parents assured me that I was and always would be their little girl and the youngest of The Harper Family. What was said at the meeting between my parents and the Head I never learned, but Lizzie told me that everyone trod on eggshells for fear of upsetting the applecart! I never again misbehaved in the music lesson or any other lesson at Grammar school and it cannot have traumatised me too much as I was not backward in coming forward in later life!

School was easy; keep the rules, be polite and helpful and greet every day with a smile; there was always someone who was worse off than yourself if you looked around! I worked hard but did not have as much natural aptitude as Lizzie and George. However, I gained 'O' and 'A' levels in their turn and went to Teacher training college in Cheltenham.

Arriving at college, I felt content with my lot and was alarmed when I discovered that life in this bigger world was more alien that I had expected. In those days, the college was in 'loco parentis' and the age of majority was not reached until you were 21. I met my first 'old broiler' at a meeting called by the warden of the hall of residence. A stern faced lady of mature years with her grey hair pulled neatly into a bun which sat into the nape of the neck, wearing dark-rimmed glasses greeted us,

"Welcome ladies. Behave well and keep the college regulations and all will be cosy for us."

Cosiness was not the word which sprang to my mind but it gave us something to laughingly discuss in the bar of the Student's Union later in the evening.

On our second day the Principal, who was a somewhat less mature lady, gave a lecture on the dangers of 'sex.'

"The best contraception is the word No," she cooed. It was difficult at eighteen not to surmise that she must have been an 'unclaimed jewel' who had not had much need to use the word in that context. The boy-men were being told at the same time to 'dig a trench' by the Vice Principal, who was also a man of the cloth. Needless to say, as it was 1968 by then, this led to half a dozen enterprising lads organising a 'dig' at midnight. The college authorities awoke to a three foot deep trench along one side of the grounds.

It caused a lot of hilarity among us students but the hierarchy were, like Queen Victoria, 'not amused.' The men were summoned to another meeting with the Vice Principal. At an opportune point the Principal herself arrived, which quietened the men at least momentarily for she lacked a sense of humour and spoke of her disgust. She ordered the offenders to fill in their trench that night so that the incident could be forgotten (although, of course, it became folk lore among the students) and that their training could commence.

CHAPTER 25

SPREADING MY WINGS

I suspect that my good nature was often exploited during my young life. I had a special friend, Veronica, at Junior School whom I always cared about, presuming that the feeling was mutual.

I continued to be a good child according to my mother and brought little anxiety onto the shoulders of my parents. I had listened to Lizzie who explained that we must always be kind and considerate, because our parents had suffered and aged far more than they had deserved.

"We shall have to make up for Stuart not being here. Will you help me?" she once asked anxiously.

"Of course I will," I assured her cuddling my older sister.

When Elizabeth left home for university I was eight years old and thought that my heart would break. I found comfort in confiding these sad feelings to my dear Mother. We wrote letters every week and my drawings went willingly to my big sister, accompanying the news from our Mother and Father. The latter's contribution usually consisted of a few lines at the end of his wife's newsy epistle! In the absence of my beloved Lizzie, Veronica became more special to me and my new confidante. We often went to each other's houses and our mothers took turns in chauffering the friend back to their appropriate coop. Beryl liked her husband to find only she and her last chick in the kitchen when he returned from work. After a hard day at the shop she knew that he would prefer not to have anyone beyond the brood in his house.

There did not appear to be any jealousy between we girls and we both enjoyed dancing classes and Brownies. Veronica was good at competitive outdoor games and was generally more robust than me. I was tiny and slight for my years and described as a dainty, graceful mover. When we both passed the 11 plus scholarship, our mothers were ecstatic. It meant that we could both go on the school bus together while they relaxed knowing that we had each other to lean on. Within the second month of attending Grammar School in 1961 Veronica announced that she had found a new friend but that we could travel to and from school sitting together. I didn't know how to react. Should I cry? Shrug my shoulders? Make waves? Be accepting? When I told Mother what had happened, she sensibly explained that growing up opened some doors and let in wonderful opportunities. As we had been separated into different classes it was inevitable that new friendships would develop and such things broadened our minds and horizons.

By the end of the month, I had been invited to tea at two girls' houses and Beryl found herself entertaining a girl called Susan who was a border at the school; the first of many exeat visits. Susan and I remained firm friends and over the teenage years we enjoyed weekends at her parents, who lived just outside Reading in a glorious house set in its own grounds, during the school holidays.

Much to my horror, at the end of the Sixth Form Susan told me that as our paths were parting completely (she was off to London for secretarial training hoping to work abroad, using her French and German while I was heading to Cheltenham) she felt that it would be better if we started afresh where friendships were concerned.

"Not even cards at birthdays and Christmas?" I asked incredulously.

"Oh. We can send those if you like but we'll be miles apart and will have little to spare for travelling and...I expect we'll make a new group of friends. That always happened in the boarding house when there was a change of personnel."

I suddenly saw red as the penny dropped. "I see. So, our family were convenient when you needed a break from school or your parents were abroad? Why do I feel used?" I snapped at my 'dearest' friend.

"Well, that's silly," replied Susan. "We've had years of special friendship and TONS of memories. You're just being childish."

"No I'm not. Friendship means commitment and commitment means forever. I can't believe that you've come to this conclusion. I don't feel there's much point in continuing a 'friendship' based only on cards."

"O.K. If that's how you feel. So be it." With that she stormed off.

I was devastated. Should I run after her and catch her before she reached the Boarding House? Her parents would collect her tomorrow and take her back to Reading. Perhaps she'd write; she knew the address having been to our house often enough! No doubt she envisaged getting in with a trendier London set. Perhaps my family did not live up to her aspirations, what with her father having a uniform covered with plentiful gold braid. I decided to share this problem with my Mother. Why did I always have to cry over everything? I must try to toughen up my heart before I reached Cheltenham. When I went to Training College to study for my B.Ed, I decided I would be circumspect with my new friendships. I was determined not to get in too deep with my peers, who always seemed to move on and hurt me in the end. I was not then sufficiently mature to realize that life changes, people grow, and friends can exist for years even if visits are only infrequent. In this day and age, this age of technology, friends are only a text, email or phone call away.

I hardened my heart. I fear other people had to 'tread on eggshells' around me during my college years. I kept everybody at arms' length and worked conscientiously for my degree but I forgot to enjoy life as a student. I suspect that I may have been a self-righteous pain to other people although some smiled politely and engaged me in conversation in the refectory or bar. My social life at College was limited but I was not particularly concerned. During the holidays, my Mother ordered me to go to the pub at the weekends as she feared that I would become lonely, even obsessive. Saturdays were busy so I opted for Fridays telling my parents that the weekend started then for students. I enjoyed my trips home, especially if Mum had organised a family get together when my nephews and niece turned up with their parents. I'm certain that my college peers would not have recognised me as the Judith Harper they knew if they had visited on these occasions.

I enjoyed learning, lectures, and tutorials and gained my degree at the end of the four years. All my teaching practices had gone well and I felt confident to face the world of work. I secured my first post at Monks Park, Bristol, a decent Comprehensive. Its Headteacher was a church elder at the Presbyterian church in Redland and there was a good 'christian ethos' there which meant a lot to me. It felt good to be alive.

CHAPTER 26

STARTLING REVELATIONS

As my 21st birthday had fallen during my third year examinations it was not properly recognised until I went home during the summer holidays. Mum had organised a Family Celebration for my coming-of-age, or getting the 'key of the door' as Grandad Harper laughingly described it so I was expecting a memorable occasion.

How right I was!

It started well as I had lovely presents from my sister, Lizzie, brother George and their families; cushions and curtains for the home that I would make when I completed my B.Ed. My parents gave me a golden box containing a set of car keys for a red Mini.

"It's just to make sure you come home and see them sometimes," teased George.

"Well, that would be a blessing," agreed Mother.

Grandad gave me some money to "Buy something nice, my love." I felt completely overwhelmed.

"What a wonderful lot you are," I said, hugging them all.

The children were put to bed after the present giving, which left the adults to enjoy the rest of the evening together. When everyone was settled in the sitting room, Mum smiled, saying,

"And we have something else. We sent most of your cards on the day but felt that we should all be together to open this one."

"Whatever can it be?" I enquired.

"Do you remember Mr and Mrs Malvern," asked Dad.

"Yes. Grandma Smith's friends."

"Well, they are a bit more than that," began Mum.

"You won't acknowledge them as such," said Lizzie, as she approached my side and grabbed my hand.

"What is it?" I asked impatiently.

"Well dear, you know that you are our adopted daughter," said Mother.

"These people are your natural grandparents," interrupted father.

"Ah," I said, sitting down on the piano stool, which was the only vacant seat in the vicinity.

There was a long silence.

"They aren't my grandparents anyway, even if they think they are," I blurted out. " They don't have any rights to me...do they?" I looked around at these adoring adorable people. "I'm yours aren't I?"

"Of course you are," said Lizzie who always knew the right words to say.

"Legally you are ours and always shall be," reassured Dad. "But now that you are an adult you can investigate your background, perhaps even meet your natural mother."

"I don't think so," I interjected indignantly.

"Well come and have a look at this lovely photograph album that Mrs Malvern has made for you," encouraged my Mother.

I picked up the parents' latest dog, a corgi called Cola, and cuddled him close to me. The pages of the album were beautifully covered with photographs of a young woman-from birth to one taken at a new year's party recently, in 1971.

"This is your natural mother. She's called Elizabeth," said Mother approvingly, showing me the picture of a small baby.

"How dare she have the same name as my darling Lizzie?" I asked completely irrationally.

"They call her Elizabeth or if they shorten it, Eliza, so not the same as our Lizzie?" soothed Father. "Now come on Judith. Try and be reasonable about this. You're an adult now. It was done with the best possible intentions and I'm sure that Mrs Malvern thought it was better for you. They are nice people you know?"

"O.K." I said in a more conciliatory manner.

My mother turned the pages, sharing a running commentary which she had presumably parroted from the words of Mrs Malvern. The photographs captured the moment and gave me a picture of the woman who had given birth to me 21 years previously.

"Why did she give me away?" I asked, knowing that my parents would have an answer.

"She didn't want to marry the man who was your father and as she was still studying she wanted to give you a better start in life than she could. Mrs Malvern was with Elizabeth when you were born.

She tried to persuade her daughter to let her have you but Elizabeth signed all the legal documents before her mother could interfere. We were so lucky to have you. We wanted a child at this time and you came to us to be our baby when you were just six weeks old."

"What a right pain you were at first," laughed George lightening the atmosphere.

"I don't want to make contact with this woman. Surely, she can't want to see me either after all this time...?" I asked, praying that this was the last thing on her mind.

"Oh no, I don't think so. When her parents asked Robert to look for you..."

"What? Robert Halford?"

"Yes dear. Turned out that he was a Private Investigator employed by Bernard and Stella Malvern," explained my father.

"Goodness. No wonder he was always here," I snorted.

"Yes. He did his job very thoroughly, didn't he?" smiled Mother.

"Anyway. You were saying. He was paid to look for me," I prompted.

"Yes. Your mother would not have anything to do with this venture. Apparently, she said that this was something that had happened years ago and her life had moved on."

"Very sensible of her too," suggested Lizzie.

"It must be awful to have further upset if one roots up the past," agreed George.

He really had changed once he grew up and at times I felt almost sisterly towards him. Directing us to the next page in the album, Lizzie said,

"Oh look. This one must be of her brothers with their mother."

"They have pots of money," said Mother. "And could obviously always afford seaside holidays and cars when we were really struggling."

"Ah, but I bet we're much happier than they are," teased my Father. "I know that Bernard felt that he wasn't much of a husband or father at one time. He even admitted to me that he was always trying to make an extra buck instead of cherishing his chicks like I did."

"That's true," said my sister in law, Belinda. "I'm always telling George how lucky he is to have a family like this one."

"Yes," agreed Thomas. "Thank goodness that we all feel that we belong together.

"Our hen house is big enough. Even space to have a young man here when you're ready, Judith."

"Not for a while then," I answered, squeezing my father's arm. "What else is there about Elizabeth Malvern?" I asked, diverting the conversation away from my lack of suitors and romance.

Mother turned back to the album. "Well, here she is in Switzerland. Stella told me that they sent her to Finishing School and then she travelled around Europe for a year. Very grand I must say!"

"Just your cup of tea Mum," said George smiling affectionately at her.

"Well yes. But... I met your Father!"

"Far better than Finishing Schools and trips to Europe," he laughed in reply.

"Here she is with Alec. I think he may be your father, Judith."

"Oh," I said showing a little interest. At least the man was rather handsome and had a tinge of red in his hair that mine showed in the sunlight.

"They make a fine looking couple," remarked my father approvingly. "No wonder they produced such a beauty."

"Oh Dad, you're such a darling," I purred.

Lizzie and George looked on admiringly both at ease with the situation. They both knew that I would never be anything except a Harper!

"There aren't many more photos. An official one at her graduation, a few holiday snaps over the years and this one taken at a New Year's do."

George smiled. "Oh yes. We'll have to keep an eye open for her."

"Don't ever say anything to her, will you?" I pleaded anxiously.

"Of course not. It's completely up to you, Judith," assured my father, as mother closed up the album.

"Anyway, it was a lovely present, wasn't it?"

"Yes, I suppose someone must have put plenty of thought into it. Will you keep it here? I'd rather not have it to hand and if I ever change my mind and think I'd like to meet her I'll have it then."

I put Cola on his cushion near the hearth and squeezed my mother's hand whispering, "Thank you."

"Of course, my love. It's completely your decision. Now, let's have a glass of champagne and toast our young woman." Father commandeered Lizzie to help him pour and distribute. The rest of the celebration went off without incident until I decided that I must go up 'wooden hill' to get my 'beauty sleep.' I lay in bed, wondering if my life was going to change now that I had learned about my 'roots'. As I drifted off to sleep, I knew that I could never in my mind and heart be anything other than a member of the Harper family.

CHAPTER 27

MOVING ON

In the September after my 21st birthday, Elizabeth Malvern became the Headteacher of Saint Mary Redcliffe Comprehensive School in the centre of Bristol close to the beautiful, Gothic church, whose magnificent outline dominated the roof-scapes.

Merrywood School had become comprehensive and was very different from the institution that Elizabeth had led since 1966. She decided that if comprehensive education was to be the name of the game, she would leave her niche in Merrywood and explore new avenues. Saint Mary Redcliffe would attract families where the parents were making a positive choice and would not be too much of a shock to her system.

A year later, I settled myself into a one bedroomed flat in Bristol, as I had been offered the post at Monks Park. With my sister's help I chose simple furniture and decorated it with the soft furnishings that I had received on my 21st. It was a cosy sensation sitting there surrounded by the loving gifts from my family. I could use the car or get to school on a bus. Sometimes, I used the bus thankfully, particularly when cash was short and payday was still a long way off. Cars eat fuel! When it rained or snowed, I was glad to use public transport rather than struggle on the wet and icy roads although I was delighted with my red Mini.

With the money that Grandpa had given me I had bought a real leather handbag. It was the just the right shape and size to take a set of books, a pencil case, a mark book and a preparation book, as well as a diary, purse and small photo album. My official title at school was ' teacher of Religious Education,' but my timetable was filled with three lessons of English and two of Physical Education. The children were reasonably well behaved (there's aways the odd horror, isn't there?)and I soon grew to love them. I spent hours trying to make my lessons interesting and inspiring. In those days visual aids were all home made, so I cut up magazines and found newspaper articles that could be mounted on black backing paper and become an aide-memoir for hungry minds. There was no googling resources then! I took books home to mark most nights, so there was rarely a spare moment; not that I found this a problem.

There was only one member of the staff who looked to cause upset as often as she could and colleagues spent their time being very careful of what they said and how they said it to her, 'treading on eggshells' for fear of a rebuff. She ruled the staffroom and obviously used her formidable manner to manipulate situations. I thought that this was, at the least, unprofessional and, at times, cruel. She decided to 'attack' me one day, so instead of capitulating to her whim, I retaliated politely but firmly. She immediately backtracked and made a conciliatory remark. From that time onwards we became firm friends and were in contact for years after I had left Monks Park!

As my faith was still important to me, I attended the local church on a Sunday morning unless I was visiting Mum and Dad at home. There were some pleasant people in the congregation and I also started going to the monthly Ladies' Fellowship group. Although I was the youngest member of the group by about 35 years this didn't seem to matter a bit as there were interesting speakers and it was very spiritual which appealed to me. I expect I was perceived as odd for my age especially as there was no other adult between 18 and 40 in the entire congregation! The minister tried to persuade me to help with the Fellowship of Youth but I didn't want to commit to their weekly meeting high in the Tower room and get involved with yet more teenagers. After all I had enough of them at school. It was a different relationship from that of teacher/pupil but I lacked the confidence at that stage to take on the venture.

Three and half years into my career I received a memo from the Head asking me to go and meet with him in my Tuesday non-teaching time. Although I knew him from church I still felt quite nervous.

"Good morning Miss Harper," was his opening remark as i stepped into his office. "How are you getting on this year?"

"Very well, thank you. I think."

"You are enjoying your work?"

"Oh yes thank you," I replied enthusiastically, " the children seem very receptive."

Miss Hewitt was the deputy for whom most people showed enormous respect as she appeared to be quite ferocious. I had noticed her watching me teach through the glass panel in my door and she always smiled at me when we passed in the corridors.

The Head continued, "Miss Hewitt has been very impressed with you and suggests that it is time you begin to look for a more challenging position; perhaps as Head of Department." He smiled benignly at me.

"Ah. I see. What would that entail?" I asked sheepishly.

"She will help you with your applications. The 'Times Educational Supplement' is there in the staffroom so have a perusal of it when you are in there. You have been a valuable member of our staff. One whom we shall miss, but it's time for you to branch out now. O.K.?" he asked rising from behind his desk and making towards the door.

The interview had clearly been terminated.

"Thank you Sir," I replied.

I was alone in my classroom. Miss Hewitt being that complimentary was unheard of; I would certainly look in the Times Educational Supplement and see what jobs were on offer. Head of Department; something I had dreamt about but not now, perhaps in four or five years. I shook myself; firstly I had to obtain that position!

After school had finished, I stayed in my teaching room marking books and acknowledging goodnights from various people going home. When I decided that the coast was clear I went down to the staffroom which was on the ground floor next to the Year Heads' office. The T.E.S. was spread open on the central coffee table and somebody had clearly been looking at Music jobs. I picked up the paper and sat in my favourite chair, facing the door to see if anybody entered. I turned the pages to the always short section headed Religious Education and glanced through the advertisements. There was a Head of Department's job in Worcester and it looked interesting, but I was not sure that I wanted to leave my flat or the area which I loved. I decided that I would discuss it with Miss Hewitt and see how it went from there.

I slept on it and dropped a note to Miss H. the next day. She came to see me later and suggested that I went to her office in my non-teaching time on Thursday afternoon.

She had the Times Educational Supplement open in front of her and said, " I presume the job in Worcester is of interest to you?"

"Yes, I think so. I need to talk it through with someone and the Head said that you were prepared to help me out."

"Certainly dear," she said, like a mother hen.

I wondered why everyone treated her as if she might bite. I always found her as amenable as she was on this occasion.

"Do you think that I've got enough experience to run a department?" I asked.

"Your relationship with the pupils you teach is good, so you should be able to crack any discipline problems. You seem to know how to diffuse and how to counteract difficult situations. You have good subject knowledge and I'm quite sure you are capable of keeping abreast of new materials and approaches. Furthermore, you get on well with your colleagues and they respect you."

"Thank you. That's very kind."

"I mean it. You may think you're locked away in a cocoon in a classroom but walls have ears. And, pupils talk about their teachers and lessons."

"To you?" I asked incredulously.

"Not usually directly, no, but I keep my ears and eyes open. You'd be amazed how freely pupils discuss their teachers' approaches to their subject and how they deal with difficult pupils and situations. Corridors are wide open spaces and attract chattering pupils during any breaks in the day," she smiled.

"So what do you think would be the best approach for me?"

"Draft out a letter of application explaining firstly why you are interested in the position (mention the opportunity to develop), secondly why you are the person that the Head should approach saying that you have good knowledge of the subject and think you could lead a group of teachers, thirdly how you would lead and develop that department, by example and sharing approaches that you have found worked and anything else about you that they might value. Do you attend a church?"

"Oh yes. Regularly."

"So talk about your faith and what you do in your church. Even if you don't get this job you should get an interview and that will be valuable experience. Bring me your completed application letter and I'll look it over with my critical eye." She paused and laughed gently. "You should also send for the application form from the school which will need filling in with details that only you know. It never fails to amaze me that Heads need to know what 'O' and 'A' levels candidates have; they rarely ask to see anyone actually teach. After all you could be the most highly qualified academic and have no teaching ability... No, I'll have to get off that high horse. Think carefully and let me know if you're going ahead with the application. I think you should. You have much potential."

With this, she got up and directed me to leave. I gathered my thoughts ready for the last session of the afternoon. Last lessons always provided a difficult challenge, but I would keep back anybody who had played me up. The pupils usually cooperated and wanted to learn-or gave that impression at least!

I applied for the job in Worcester but was not successful although I enjoyed the interview as an experience and had some positive feedback from the Deputy Head. When I spotted the Head of Religious Education at Saint Mary Redcliffe's, I put in another application.

I was interviewed by a whole team of people; the Chair of Governors, the vicar of the church, his Vice Chair, a retired businessman, the Deputy Head (who went by the name of Mirabelle Dobson), the Senior Master (Brian Baxter, who only looked up once from his folder to ask me about my love of music) and an attractive woman who was Personal Secretary to the Headteacher. This last person was a surprising addition to the interviewing panel but she was standing in for the Head who had been summoned to her seriously ill mother's bed side.

This time I was offered the job. What excitement! When I went home at the weekend my parents were overjoyed. My mother was still writing weekly but I had made little of the application as she tended to get things out of perspective. Her disappointment that I hadn't become head of Department at the first attempt had been sad to experience, despite Dad explaining that if I had been successful I would have ended up at the other end of the M5! This time, I had decided not to lay my heart open for once as I really wanted this post. I was going to be able to stay in my flat and visit them regularly, of which Mother heartily approved.

CHAPTER 28

PATHS CONVERGING

Sometimes the penny is slow to drop. I had seen on headed correspondence that the Head of 'my new school' was a lady called Elizabeth Malvern, followed by her copious qualifications, but as she was referred to by her colleagues as 'Libby' I never expected to see the woman who greeted me on September 4th 1976 on my first morning at Saint Mary Redcliffe School.

I think that I managed to suppress my surprise. Standing before her assembled staff in the glorious staffroom allocated to us, was the person who had appeared in the New Year photograph and as the central character in the rest of the album compiled by Stella Malvern for my 21st birthday. I was somewhat horrified; I was going to be working for my natural mother!

As Head of Department I attended meetings with Libby, her deputies Mirabelle and Brian and the other Heads of Department. At the end of the Autumn term, the Head suggested that the twelve of us went out for a meal together. She chose a quiet place on Park Street in the centre of Bristol, paid for our meal, saying that this was our Christmas present and made a touching speech about not being able to run the school without excellent leadership in departments. She really was a lovely person and I soon grew to like her a lot.

I decided to send her a Christmas card and signed it 'Judith.' At the meal she had dropped formal titles and I thought it appropriate to use my first name. The next day there was a card waiting in my pigeon hole in the staffroom which was signed 'Libby' with a short message which read, 'thank you for all your hard work.' There was nothing special about this as all the staff had received a card but I still felt pleased to have it.

Christmas, 1976 at home was the usual fun-loving time. We exchanged presents and my nephews and niece were old enough to participate in card games. I was asked lots of questions about my new job which I answered with relish. Everyone was very supportive over it but when we washed up after tea on Christmas Day, Dad asked me about my social life. I laughed and told him that I was having a lovely time with my colleagues and was busy and satisfied with my work.

"When you're ready Dear," he said, "but don't forget we are not getting any younger."

"I'll try to find someone," I replied, giving him a hug." It's hard to find someone who comes up to your high standards."

He beamed with delight and then he mentioned Bernard Malvern whose wife was very ill. I kept my thoughts to myself although I was surprised that nobody had talked about Libby's mother at school.

I started attending the church next to the school. The Church of England is different from a Free Church but we all worship the same God and I had been used to an Anglican church in my childhood in the village. There seemed to be a lot more children attending Saint Mary Redcliffe and I found the atmosphere conducive to worship and prayer. The Sunday School was thriving and I was encouraged by its leader to teach in it. I explained that I thought the children would be glad of a break from me as I taught some of them in the week for Religious Education. Anyway, it seemed right to be witnessing to the pupils who were attending services and went to the school. I wanted them to see me as a member of the congregation not only as their teacher.

I expect this was asking too much of them. Once a teacher, always a teacher!

CHAPTER 29

IS BLOOD THICKER?

Relationships are like eggs. They can be easily cracked, easily broken, squashed and made useless. Elizabeth had not looked for other liaisons since Alec and the baby. She had made a conscious decision to put all her energy into work and the pupils. She felt that she must be hopeless when it came to forming proper attachments to other people if she couldn't even confide to her boyfriend that she was pregnant with his child. She thought that she had loved Alec which is why she had allowed him to sleep with her. Once she was pregnant, the thought of spending the rest of her life with him was quite untenable, so it could have only been 'desire' not 'love' that had fueled their relationship.

Even when invited out, Elizabeth could smile and thank the 'nice young man' (a useful phrase for her parents when they started probing into her life) but say she wasn't able to go on dates as there was just too much pressure of work. She usually managed to find a friend to go to the theatre with her and was often seen there or at the cinema or a gig with a female companion. Susan had been her deputy at the Girls' Grammar School in Bristol and had known her for years. Although her closest friend, Elizabeth always skimmed over her relationship with Alec and never confided that she had given birth to a daughter. Elizabeth always hoped that only she and her mother now knew of the heartbreaking decision that she had been forced to make all those years ago. Then, of course, her mother had fallen ill and confided in her father. She could not believe even now that they had employed a private investigator to search for her baby and found her successfully. Despite not wanting to be part of their scheme, she could not help being interested in the information which had been revealed in this nefarious way. Elizabeth insisted that she had no wish to meet her daughter, see any photographs of her or even hear anything about her. It was all a long time ago and another life.

Fortunately, her parents had reluctantly accepted these wishes, although they told her that they still intended to stay friendly with the adoptive parents and thus have nominal contact with their grandchild.

"Whatever you want," said Elizabeth in a disinterested manner when she was informed of their intentions, "but don't come and tell me anything; I don't want to know."

"O.K.," agreed Stella who found it almost impossible to comprehend her daughter's position. Bernard had warned her to tread very softly in the situation, as he knew that his precious daughter could be very forceful. He had no intention of alienating her from the family and realized that life must have been very difficult for her even if she had never fully confided this to them.

The closest relationships that Elizabeth developed were with her colleagues. She had retained contact with Mabel who had lectured with her, and Betty who had shared her student room in university. Even the latter, however, did not know about the existence of the baby although they had first met only a couple of months after the adoption. During her 5 years as Head of Merrywood Girls, Elizabeth had kept a working relationship with her two deputies and her secretary, but only one, Susan, was part of her friendship group. She felt that the only thing which she had in common with many of her colleagues was education and that relaxing with them away from school would be hopeless.

When Judith arrived at Saint Mary Redcliffe Libby found herself strangely drawn towards her newest recruit. She spent the first term appraising her; watching her deal with children and staff. Liking the things she was observing she decided to invite the younger woman over for lunch one Saturday.

"Oh. How kind of you. I'll have to see which one is free," I had replied hoping that my face and body language did not reveal the turbulence in my stomach.

At home I thought carefully about my response to this situation. Ought I to discuss the problem with somebody else? I decided that Mother would be a complete nightmare and as she was fond of Libby's mother would be likely to let that particular cat out of its bag.

I decided that Lizzie must continue in her usual role as my confidante. I dialed my sister's number. She picked up.

"Hello Lizzie."

"Hello you," she replied, "how are you then?"

"Fine. How about you?"

"Yes, everything is great with me. The kids are good although Emma has a bit of a cough, the remains of a nasty cold which spread through the whole family after the New Year. Are you fit? No bugs from the kids or anything?"

"No." I laughed. "I think you become immune eventually, working in schools, unless there's a new strain of 'flu or something."

"Good. I'm glad that you're O.K. Have you talked to Mum recently?"

"Last Saturday. They seemed all right. Has anything changed?"

"No. I'm just so glad that you keep in touch with them so regularly."

"Lizzie, can I talk something important through with you?"

"Of course, Darling. Can I phone you back in half an hour 'though when I've put James to bed."

"O.K. Thanks Lizzie. Bye for now."

I tried not to think about the situation or make a plan about what I would say. I couldn't settle to doing anything and was relieved when the phone made a welcoming ring.

"Hello Judith," said my sister's warm voice. "Now what can I do for you?"

"I've got a real dilemma. You see, I didn't say anything at Christmas but I've known something ever since I started at Saint Mary R's."

"Gosh, now you've intrigued me. What is it that you've known and not shared?"

"That the Head of my school is also my MOTHER?"

"Goodness....and how do you feel about that? How can you be sure? Does she know you're her daughter?"

"I'm O.K. with it. I think. Her name is Elizabeth Malvern and she looks identical to the photograph of her that we saw taken at the New Year!"

"But, does SHE realise who you are?"

"Oh no. I don't intend that she should ever know. As far as I can tell nobody at all knows about her past and she never discusses anything personal."

"So in that case, what's your dilemma?"

"Well, she's invited me over to her house for lunch one Saturday and I don't know whether to go or not."

" Won't she think it really odd if you don't go?"

"I expect so, but how am I going to cope?"

"Just treat her like any other work colleague. Don't mention the fact that you are adopted but talk about your family as you would normally. In fact, just be yourself and act naturally. She'll be bound to love you anyway!"

"Well, think about me."

"When are you going to go there?"

"Probably the second Saturday of next month. Don't want to think about it too long."

"You must let me know how it goes."

"Don't say anything to anyone, especially Mum and Dad."

"Not even Thomas?"

"O.K. That's different but you must both promise not to say anything to anyone else. If the parents get to hear, they'll probably tell the Malverns and then Mrs M. will tell Libby. I couldn't bear it all coming out like that you see."

"Don't worry my love. We'll keep this to ourselves and won't talk about it in front of the children. Trust us."

"Oh, I do. I don't know whether I'm excited, frightened or how to react. It could be a bit of an ordeal. Thanks for listening and advising. What would I do without you?"

"That's fine. Now, just calm down, make your cocoa, read your book or do your marking. Then go to bed and don't let it keep you awake."

"I will, Lizzie. Give my love to Thomas and the children. 'Bye, and thank you."

"That's O.K. Take care. 'Bye."

I felt better. After a decent night's sleep I went into school and when I found Libby, I thanked her for the invitation and arranged to visit on the second Saturday of the month.

The meal, which was the first of many, went very well and we found lots to talk about to each other. We had similar tastes in music and theatre and started going to performances together. One evening after a good meal and a lovely bottle of wine in a restaurant, Libby invited me back to her flat for coffee. Perhaps she'd had more than usual to drink but she suddenly started to tell me about her life. Before I knew what was happening she had told me all about Alec, whom she thought was her true love and how when she became pregnant she realized that she did not want to keep the baby that she was carrying. I faked surprise at this news.

"Goodness, whatever did you do?"

"I knew I was too young. Alec wanted to travel after university, the same as me, so I told him I was finishing the relationship."

"Did he know about the baby?"

"Oh no. The only person I told about that was Mum and I made her promise to not even say anything to my father."

"Why ever not?"

"He would have been furious. Probably would have killed Alec, if not both of us."

This sounded a bit melodramatic so I prompted, "So what happened?"

"The baby was born in a London Hospital and taken to the adoptive parents almost immediately."

"What did you feel then?"

"Devastated at first...but I'm sure that it was for the best."

"Do you ever still think about her?" I asked tentatively.

"Of course I do! But I don't dwell on it. A lot of water's gone under the bridge since then."

"Is that why you became a workaholic?" I smiled.

"I expect so. The problem was that my Mother told my Father and they started a search for her in 1955."

"That's 20 years ago!" I laughed.

"Yes, but I often wonder if they still have any contact?"

"Haven't you asked them?"

"No. I told them I didn't want to know the details."

"And they never told you any?"

"No. I do wonder sometimes. I suppose she would be around your age."

She became pensive and quiet and it felt like my cue to leave. I got up and collected my bag and jacket.

"Don't say anything about this, will you Judith?"

"Of course not."

"I'm sorry to burden you with all of this. I've never told anyone about it before. Can't think why it came out tonight."

"Must be the wine," I laughed, planting a kiss on her cheek. "Your secret's safe with me. Get yourself to bed and I'll take a taxi home. See you on Monday. Enjoy your day of rest."

"Thank you," Libby replied, hugging me. "Don't work too hard tomorrow."

"No fear of that. I'm off to church and there's a do to meet the new curate after the service. Goodnight Libby."

"Goodnight Judith."

I escaped feeling pleased. I had managed to stay quite calm and positive while my mother confided in me about my own birth. At least she confessed that she had thought about me on and off over the years.

The next morning turned out to be the start of a new era for me. The new curate, Simon Hutchinson, proved to be a delightful young man from Gloucestershire. He had graduated from Keble College and had trained for the ministry nearby at Ripon College, Cuddesdon. After his ordination, Simon had worked for a year at Saint Martin in the Fields in London. He worked with the homeless and was involved with the cafe in the Crypt. In 1977 he was offered the post in Bristol. A couple of months into his ministry he asked me if I would be interested in setting up a youth club. I thought and prayed about it and decided that now I was confident and established in my teaching career it would be an extension of my role with children and a good thing to do. I was becoming conscious that I liked Simon a lot and that running a youth club would give me plenty of opportunities to be with him. I confided my feelings to Libby. After all, she had shared her greatest secret with me!

"It sounds a lovely idea, Judith. If I came to church would you introduce me to him?"

"You're sounding like my mother," I teased.

"No. Older sister, or best friend even," she replied without a moment's hesitation.

"Yes. That's better! Come to lunch next Sunday after we've been to 11 o'clock."

"What a champion idea," she replied.

So it was that the woman who had given birth to me was the first person to properly meet the man who was to become the love of my life.

The Youth Club was born. It was to run after evensong on Sundays. Simon had the knack of speaking to young people, talking to them as grown-ups but at the same time insisting on politeness and good behaviour.

"Jesus loves us all. You should always treat other people with love and consideration," he announced at our first meeting. The wonderful thing about him was that he did exactly this and treated everyone the same. To me it was clearly apparent that the Spirit worked through him. The youth club was a great success with the young and most people were thrilled at its progress. Naturally, success caused some to find their feathers ruffled. Miriam was a hard worker in the parish, but one learned to be careful with her. She had a tendency to dominate and treat everybody, including Simon, as 'though they were inferior to her.

One day, Simon retaliated when Miriam started to criticise two of the older boys who attended the youth club.

"I saw them smoking at the corner of Redcliffe Hill the other day and it gives the church a bad name."

"Did anyone else know that they belonged to our church?" asked Simon.

"No. But I did - and it's disgusting."

"I don't remember Our Lord saying such a thing," replied Simon gently.

"That was then and this is now. God wouldn't like it."

"Oh Miriam! Do you have a direct line to the Almighty?"

"No but it's not right," she carried on insisting.

"Remember, 'judge not as ye be not judged' and 'let he who is without sin throw the first stone.'"

"That's right. Resort to scripture," she snapped, " You vicars are all the same."

"Indeed," replied Simon, " that's the word of God."

Apparently Miriam turned on her heel and stormed away muttering to herself. For once she looked defeated. When Simon told me about his encounter with her I laughingly said, " Gosh. Did you set out to make her feel small?"

"Not really, but I'm irritated that people tread on eggshells with her all the time. We have to encourage people to stand up for their beliefs and not let her browbeat them."

"Easier said than done if you're a mere parishioner."

"Do you really think she backed down because of the collar?" asked Simon incredulously.

"Of course," I smiled. "People like Miriam have some respect for the clergy if not for the rest of us."

"Oh well I never," he replied.

Poor Simon. He was almost too naive for this world. However, the more I saw him at work, the more I realized that he was special. The youth club members adored him. The teenage girls flirted with him and the boys hung on his words. It helped that he was sporty- football, table tennis, badminton, tennis, cricket and he was always fair but competitive which they appreciated.

After one of our Sunday evening meetings, Simon suggested that we had ' a date.'

" Nothing too heavy," he said.

"Of course not," I replied.

"You're on holiday, aren't you?"

"Yes," I smiled encouragingly, thinking of the relief in being less stressed and away from the classroom.

"Shall we take a picnic to Brandon Hill on Tuesday then? It's my day off and the weather looks quite promising."

"Oh, that would be lovely."

"We can walk over Redcliffe Bridge, through Queens Square, across the Tramway Centre, past the Royal hotel and the Cathedral, up Park Street, into Berkeley Square and then through to Brandon Hill."

"My, you have done your homework," I teased.

"Well, do you think it's a good idea?"

"Of course I do. We must pray for good weather."

"Meet me outside the church at around 11 then. Don't forget the picnic. I've got a gabardine which we can sit on."

"Oh good. I'll bring some Lemon Barley. I've got a really good flask that I can cool down with cold water before I fill it. I'll bring some coffee too so that will make a change."

"We'll make a day of it and get to know each other better. O.K?"

"Yes. Lovely!" I smiled.

Simon touched me on the arm, "See you at 11 on Tuesday," he said tenderly.

"Yes. I'm looking forward to it already."

I returned to my flat on Cloud 9. Once I was indoors I longed to tell someone. With whom should I share my excitement. My parents? My sister? My mother cum older sister cum best friend? In the end I chose Lizzie. She had always been there; my confidante for my whole life. One who would never judge me. She, in fact, encouraged me but warned me not to let him know I was so keen. Some hope...

CHAPTER 30

PICNICS AND MORE

Our first date was all that I had ever dreamed of. Simon was kind and attentive, made no demands and yet was obviously as keen on me as I was on him. At the end of the afternoon we walked back to my flat in Hampton Road.

"You ought to move nearer to the church and school than this," suggested Simon. "South of the river would be cheaper for you and there are some lovely houses in Southville."

"I'll have to see about that," I replied tentatively.

"Yes," he smiled, "I suppose a lot depends on how things work out. Talking of which, would it be O.K. if we did something like this again?"

"Well, I have another two Tuesdays before the Autumn term starts, but then it will be all systems go for the new school year."

"Right. We'll make a date for next Tuesday. If the weather is reasonable we'll picnic again but if not we'll think of something else. Give a 'wet weather date' some thought and let me know your ideas next Sunday."

He smiled again, touched me on the arm and turned away to return to his flat in the Vicarage. Naturally, I was quickly on the phone to Lizzy. I could tell she was smiling as I poured out the details of our day together.

"Can you think of something we can do if it rains?" I asked her.

"I suggest a picnic at one of your flats," she suggested.

"That's a good idea. An indoor picnic. It'll have to be at mine as I don't suppose he'll want the vicar to get wind of our liaison yet."

"Liaison! Oh, is that what it is?"

"Well, friendship then if you prefer it."

"I think liaison sounds a lot more interesting! I'm sure it's going to develop into more than friendship my sweet," said my big sister tenderly. " I hope he's as smitten as you are," she added with some concern in her voice.

"Oh, I think he is. He was quick to suggest we met next week and called it a date," I purred.

"Good. That's what I like to hear. Most encouraging."

The rest of the phone call was Lizzie talking about the children and Thomas. I was not really taking much notice. My mind was far too concerned with the new love in my life.

I met Libby on Friday as she'd phoned me to invite me to Bell's Diner in York Road which had not been open long. We talked about what we had done in our holidays. She had been abroad to France and was very full of all the places which she had visited.

"So, what have you been doing dear?" she asked.

"Well," I started, smiling at her, "I've had a date with the new curate at Saint Mary Redcliffe."

"Oh how lovely. What did you do?"

"We had a picnic on Brandon Hill."

"And...?"

"We're having another one next week."

"Um. He's playing it safe?" laughed Libby.

"It's when he gets his day off and it's difficult with him living at the vicarage."

"You could always invite him over to your flat."

"Yes I know but I think it will better if we take it steadily. After all he is a curate and I am an R.E. teacher at the school which is attached to that church."

" I suppose so. Although, it would be lovely if a romance was to develop," enthused my mother cum big sister cum best friend.

"We've only had one date," I laughed.

"Yes, but there'll be another next week."

"And if it rains," I added conspiratorially, " we'll have a picnic at home."

"That's more like it. Anyway, what did you talk about?"

This was not a lot different from talking with my parents but then, Libby was my mother even if she didn't know it!

Needless to say, Lizzie had told our parents about my love life. This led to a very interesting call from Mum, who told me that they were coming over at the weekend and hoped that I would introduce the new curate to them. There was nothing to lose, so I said I was looking forward to their visit.

I woke up the next morning and experienced the feelings that Joni Mitchell sings about in 'Chelsea Morning.' It was 10 past 7 and " the sun poured in like butterscotch and melted all my senses." Oh to be able to write such imagery. I waited for the alarm to 'wake' me at 8 o'clock. The joy of an extra hour in bed during the holidays!

The first meeting with Simon had gone well and now he wanted a 'date.' AND, my mother cum friend and my wonderful sister, Lizzie, seemed to be pleased for me. On top of that, my parents would meet him at the weekend. I so hoped everyone would like each other.

CHAPTER 31

GIFTS FOR THE NEEDY

For someone who didn't want to meet my birth mother I found myself in her company every day in term time, often on a couple of evenings in the week, on occasional Sunday afternoons and two or three days a week in the holidays as long as we were both in Bristol. Obviously, I saw Simon as often as possible. We had an affinity and could never stop talking or laughing except for the occasional loving kiss. In December 1977 he said,

"I won't buy you a Christmas present if you don't mind."

"Oh," I replied trying to hide immense disappointment.

"We'll just go and lap up the Christmas atmosphere in town one day nearer the 25th and then give money to the needy in lieu of presents. Alright?"

It wasn't a bit alright really but I could see that it was a Christian thing to do.

After the Christmas party for the youth club in December Simon suggested that we went to town on the Tuesday before Christmas Day. As I would have broken up on the previous Friday and it was a few days before he would be snowed under with Christmas duties, it seemed a good idea. It was a magical morning; frosty, clear and inviting. I wore my sheepskin three quarter length coat and a hat which had been last year's Christmas present from my parents and the pair of gloves that I'd been given for my birthday. One could not possibly wear heels or peep toed court shoes for such an expedition so I donned my old, well worn walking shoes which were brown and matched the gloves, hoping that Mum and Dad would give me cash for Christmas so that I could purchase some boots.

I met Simon in the Cadenita coffee shop on Baldwin Street at 10.30 (a rendezvous which we often used when going into town). I had once been kept waiting ages at the church when he had been called out to minister to a dying soul and he decided that a warm place where you could drink coffee during the wait was a more civilised arrangement. He got up to greet me and placed a kiss on my cheek; the first sign of public affection so I was rather thrilled. The cafe was adorned with streamers, a decorated Christmas tree and festive napkins on the table. There were a number of people there and the friendly bustle and hum created a jolly atmosphere there. Once we'd sat down he placed my hands between his and looked directly at me.

"You must know how I feel about you," he began.

"Yes," I smiled, " and I feel the same way."

"Do you think you could bear to be a vicar's wife?"

"Is this what I think it may be?"

"Yes, of course. I'm asking you to marry me."

There was a pause.

"You don't need to answer straight away if you need more time to consider the implications."

Consider the implications? I knew exactly what they might be but I loved him and replied, "I have no need to take time to answer. I'd be delighted to be a vicar's wife as long as that vicar is you."

"That's the answer which I have been praying for," he said leaning over to put his lips on mine. "We'll announce our engagement before you go home for Christmas then?"

"No, let's wait until after Christmas as I'd like to tell my family face to face. I shall only be away from the 23rd to the 27th. Perhaps you could come over when your duties here are finished."

"Ah. Let's see. I'll tell you what. I'll go and see my folks on Boxing Day and come over to your parent's place on the 27th. Do you have to come back to Bristol then?"

"No, I suppose not, but I'd like to be back here for the New Year."

"Could your parents put me up overnight on the 27th?"

"I should think so. I'll ask them."

"Don't tell them it's me that will be coming, say it's Libby or someone else."

My heart lurched. I didn't want to tell him my true relationship to Libby yet and then I remembered, "She's away at her parents. Her Mother's really ill so she's spending most of the holidays with them in case it's their last Christmas as a family."

"I'm sure you'll think of some plan. Now, drink up as we have to buy your Christmas present."

"I thought we weren't buying for each other, only giving to the needy."

"That's right. We are. I need you to wear a ring so that everyone knows that we intend to marry."

"Soulmates," I murmured.

"Definitely," agreed Simon.

With that we got up, straightened the chairs as if we were still in school and stepped out into the bustling streets of Christmas Bristol.

Simon had obviously done his window shopping as he took me straight to Kemp Brothers on Union Street. We looked together at the beautiful rings in the trays.

"I can't afford some of the flashier ones."

"I'd like a solitaire diamond set in gold if one isn't too expensive?"

"Why so adamant?" he teased.

"I want you to be the only man in my life and me to be the only woman in yours."

"Oh you Pickle," he laughed. "The things you say."

"Sorry. Have I said the wrong thing?"

"Not at all; it's romantic and very lovely," he replied grabbing my hand and taking me into the shop.

I was confronted with a tray of solitaire diamond engagement rings. All were set beautifully in gold, silver and what appeared to be pewter or so I thought; I found out later in life that it was white gold. I looked at Simon.

"Do you like this one?" he asked pointing to a ring in the middle row.

I presumed that he was giving me an idea of the price range within which I could choose.

"Yes," I replied, "but I prefer this one," pointing to a cheaper one below it.

"Are you sure?"

I nodded.

The assistant removed the ring from the box and placed it on my palm saying, " See if it fits?"

Simon took the ring and gingerly pushed it on to the correct finger of my left hand. " O.K.?" he asked, smiling into my eyes.

"Oh yes. It's beautiful."

"Do you wish it wrapped or is Madam going to keep it on?"

"Oh no. Have it wrapped Simon."

While the transaction was being completed I glanced around the shop. There seemed to be some fine watches which I could peruse quietly when Simon wasn't with me.

As it happened things turned out differently from the way that we had originally planned because we decided that Simon's parents needed to have us both with them when they heard our news. To make matters worse, the vicar developed a sore throat during the run up to Christmas and he struggled through the Day nursing a sore throat and, we suspected, a temperature but was forced to succumb to his illness that night. His wife had anticipated this course of events and had asked Simon if he would stand by to take the Boxing Day service and hold the fort for the rest of the day. What could he say? He phoned his parents to explain the situation and tell them that he would not be home before the 28th December. His mother was naturally disappointed and said that she would have to tolerate it.

"When I get a parish of my own, you can come and spend Christmas with me but until then I have to fit in with my boss," he explained to his more philosophical father.

"We understand my boy. Just looking forward to hearing all your news from Bristol. Shall we keep hold of your present?"

"Yes. That's the best idea. Hope you haven't got carried away this year?" Simon laughed thinking about the amount which they had generously spent last year.

"Ah. We only have you and Rachel and her family to spoil. There won't be so much once you're married and there are grandchildren to treat," he chuckled.

How had he guessed? Surely he couldn't really know about their intended engagement.

"Well son," he added interrupting Simon's thoughts, "we'll expect you on the 28th then. We'll get your sister and her children over so that we can all be together as a family."

Should he tell dad his secret? No; one more mouth to feed could hardly be a problem to a woman as well organised as his mother. She would soon get over her disappointment at him coming a day later when she met Judith and heard of their intentions.

"I'll send the card through the post," he heard Mother shout as he was saying goodbye to his father.

Simon decided that he better find a rather special card for his parents; it might soften the blow for his mother. He'd already sent cards and tokens to his sister and her family, husband Peter and the twins Mary and Martha, but now felt obliged to push the boat out a bit further for his parents. How far? He would ask Judith, but he thought a nice hamper from Lewis's in Broadmead might be a good idea-something that would also help the provisioning of the meal on the 28th, but which they would receive before Christmas.

I agreed that this was a sound assessment of the situation and offered to arrange its delivery as he was so busy. A trip into town suited me as I wanted to buy a watch as a combined Christmas and engagement present for Simon. This would be an ideal opportunity! I felt quite conspiratorial about the whole affair, knowing that Simon would not consider this trip would be my opportunity to buy a present for him.

The beautiful ring stayed nestled in its small box in a drawer in Simon's desk. I thought about it often in the days leading up to Christmas but we had decided that it should be first worn on the 27th at my parent's home when I received it as his Christmas present. At first he said that he'd wrap it up in a shoe box so that nobody would expect the true contents of his gift but then he realized that he didn't have one.

"I'll find something," he'd said.

His kind lovely face came into my mind framed by blonde hair that reached his shoulders in the style of those days turning him into Adonis in my eyes. Perhaps love blinded me, but his good looks and deep velvet voice were commented on by other members of the congregation who certainly weren't in love with him! I had always imagined myself being attracted to a taller man like my father but I fitted perfectly under his shoulder and as he stood 5 foot 10 inches he was definitely tall enough. As long as he didn't grow fat. I couldn't bear fat men or those with beards, but guessed that now I'd have a choice; don't overfeed him or let him grow a beard. Beards I'd decided, with no real experience, must be bristly and uncomfortable and their close proximity was out of the question.

Simon didn't wear his 'dog collar' unless he was on duty. His idea, which differed from Robert the vicar was: ' once ordained, always ordained, clerical collar or not.' He frequently said that nurses or surgeons would respond to a situation even when out of uniform, policemen too I supposed.

Our political views verged towards the left (which would make our dining table discussions less fractious) and we also agreed about morality, equality and concern for all people. No need to 'tread on any eggshells' with him.

In fact, it was a perfect match! Made in heaven?

CHAPTER 32

A PRESENT IN A CHALICE BOX

I returned to my parent's home on Christmas eve. Simon and I had said fond farewells after meeting for coffee and as I had packed the car with clothes and family presents I was able to drive to Horbury Markham in time for lunch. When I think about home " I miss the village green, the church, the clock, the steeple." How insightful are these words of Ray Davies. Considering he lived in North London, he showed a lot of empathy for we villagers! I wonder if Fortis Green was more like a village than I imagined. I then let my thoughts drift towards the news that we were going to tell my parents on the 27th. I felt so lucky to have found an ideal partner, but parents sometimes need more persuasion. Hopefully, Simon's love would shine from him and there would be no problems. It must be awful if parents don't care for their child's chosen life partner. I fully expected support from my brother and sister. They were both level headed and these days even George showed love and affection for everyone. Whenever I thought of my elder brother my mind turned to memories of Stuart. How happy he would have been to know that I had met my soul mate. I liked to think that he would have made a good husband for somebody too.

I turned off the main road and headed towards the village. Home! Mum and Dad were their usual excited selves as they welcomed me. The decorated tree stood majestically in the hall, holly with blood red berries was pushed behind the pictures and a sprig of mistletoe hung down from the hall light. What a perfect setting this would be to welcome Simon to on the day after Boxing day.

"You look radiant," said my father, as I embraced my parents.

I wished I could share with them why I looked so happy but hoped that they would accept that I was pleased to be home with them after a successful term and was ready to enjoy being cosseted by my family.

I was ushered into the living room where a log fire was burning brightly. The Christmas cards were hanging from a ribbon. The nuts, dates, figs and a fruit bowl, overflowing with apples and clementines, were strategically placed on a new long coffee table in the centre of the room.

"Oh, that's lovely, Mum!" I exclaimed.

"Yes, isn't it? My present this year," she smiled.

"Well, our present really, dear. You'll have a smaller personal gift when Santa comes," chuckled my father, as he slid a free arm around my excited mother.

"It's lovely to have you home, Judith," purred Mum squeezing my arm.

"Lovely to be home," I replied.

"Well come on love. I'm sure that our girl could do with a cuppa after her drive and some of that cake too," Dad said raising his voice as Mum was disappearing into the kitchen.

"Don't tell me any news until your mother has come back," commanded my father. "So what sort of journey did you have?"

"Oh fine thanks. Fortunately, the car seems to have a good nature and so far I haven't had any worries with it. One of my colleagues had an horrific bill from the garage the other day; the fuel wasn't getting through and something seized up."

"Let's hope that nothing like that happens to you."

"Like what?" asked Mum arriving with a lovely cake on a plate which had once belonged to my grandmother.

"Oh, we're only talking about cars," Dad replied.

"Well, no discussing the school or Simon until I get back with the tea," ordered Mum with a smile.

If only she knew! Visits and 'phone calls can tell the recipient a lot, but no one can see the eyes sparkling with love when recounting the stories of meetings and dates. My parents were aware of how often Simon and I saw each other. I expect that Lizzie had probably told them that she thought we were in love. Lizzie had always been a romantic; willing people to have a good life and praying that other people would be able to find the sort of happiness that she shared with Thomas.

Dad told me all the news of my nephews and niece until Mum returned with the tea.

"Well, what news is there?" she asked.

"I've had a great term and my job's going really well."

"And how's Simon?"

"Hang on Dear," interrupted my father. " Let's hear some school news first."

"Well, I've made some good friends."

"Anyone in particular?" asked Mum, smiling quizzically.

Did she know anything? Surely, Lizzie hadn't told them! I decided that I'd have to presume that she had kept my secret safe.

"I see the Head a lot," I said.

"She must be a nice woman then," smiled Dad.

"Yes. We get on really well." I decided that even Simon would be a safer subject of conversation and so added, " She met Simon very early on."

"Oh!" said Mum, almost sharply.

"Well, she was around the day after he asked me for my first proper date with him."

"Of course," answered Dad, "You're bound to be chatting to people of your own age."

I kept my own counsel at this point as my 'mother' was hardly the same age as me! Father is able to keep Mum's excesses in check and she soon recovered from her disappointment at not being the first to know about Simon.

"I'm so glad that he's coming over on the 27th. I suppose Christmas is a busy time for clergymen," she smiled.

"Yes. Advent can be busy too, preparing people for the Lord's second coming."

"Um. I suppose so," agreed Mum at this piece of theology. Although she would have been quick to tell anyone that she was a devout Christian, the liturgical significance of the church's year had not greatly encroached on her life. Perhaps it would once she had a vicar as a son in law?

"Anyway, Simon will be here on the 27th and then we will go to his parents on the 28th for a couple of days before heading back to Bristol."

"Can't you and Simon stay a bit longer?"

"Well, he won't have even seen his parents until then. The vicar has worn himself out and although he insists on doing Christmas Day services, he's asked that Simon works on Boxing Day. You'll have me until the morning of the 28th."

"Of course," answered my dad who seemed to grasp situations quicker than my dear mother.

I put my arm around her as she sat in her favourite chair and hugged her for a long time.

"Let's make the most of my visit," I said.

"Lizzie, Thomas and the children are having Christmas with us this year and your brother and his family will be here on the 27th-it's Belinda's parents' turn this Christmas."

How funny to be talking of visits as turns. I suppose every married couple has to ensure that all the balls are kept in the air and sometimes do a bit of eggshell treading to see that nobody gets hurt. Simon and I would have all this to look forward to eventually. We had not discussed our wedding plans, but I suspected that we might marry at the end of the summer term next year. I would have to ask the vicar in the village if he had any free dates in July or August 1978. Or, perhaps the vicar at Saint Mary Redcliffe, Matthew, would wish to officiate.

I helped Mum prepare a meal which the three of us ate with relish. It was customary to attend midnight communion which started at 11.45 so we left at 11.30 and made our way to the familiar church of my youth. It was decorated with some taste and more enthusiasm and everybody greeted us warmly. I always loved the Christmas crib which was in its usual place at the north side of the sanctuary steps. When midnight strikes the baby Jesus is processed through the church and placed in the empty manger. Such a poignant moment for any Christian. My thoughts went to my intended fiance and I prayed that his service would be as memorable as I knew this one would be for me.

At 11.45 the vicar announced the first processional hymn, 'Once in Royal David's City.' Christmas 1977 was the year for Stephen Bell's son, John to sing the opening verse. Stephen was one of George's old school friends. I noticed that he stood tall with pride as his eldest son sang beautifully in tune. The elderly church warden, Bob Smalling read the opening verse and the vicar intoned the prayer which introduced the intercessions: for peace, for the royal family, especially H.M the Queen who would be broadcasting to the nation

133

on the following afternoon, for the firefighters who were on a 9 week strike, for Ethiopia and Somalia who were at war, for the efforts towards nuclear disarmament and for ourselves.

The vicar and his entourage moved to the back of the church as we sang, "Oh Come all ye Faithful." After the third verse we stopped to listen to the church bells as they marked the hour of midnight. The organ wheezed into life and the choir sang lustily, "Yeah Lord we greet thee, born this happy morning." The bambino, cradled in the vicar's arms and brought to the crib during the singing of the final verse was laid in the manger. Everyone knelt in adoration and prayer. I loved this moment as my mother squeezed my arm knowingly. Christmas had begun!

We had a warm drink on our arrival home and were in bed by 1.30. The turkey was roasting slowly and smells were already wafting upwards as I drifted into a happy dreamless sleep. The church bells chiming 7 woke me. My darling Simon would be preparing to take the first communion service of Christmas day at 8 o'clock. I thanked God for him, for sending me somebody to love and for giving me a warm loving family of my own. My thoughts wandered towards Libby. On the anniversary of Christ's birth did she think of the child that she had given away? She seemed such a decent person that it was hard to associate her with a feckless act. For the first time, I began to empathise with her situation. When I was conceived she and Alec were miles away from their families and friends. Perhaps they were lonely and afraid? Perhaps they had needed somebody to lean on? Libby had implied that she knew that a permanent relationship would be too hard and had chosen to give up boyfriend and child when she found herself pregnant. Perhaps it was very frightening for her? Perhaps it was brave and mature to stand back detached from her situation? There must have been many unwanted children born onto loveless marriages. Libby had told me that she often thought about her child which was a comfort to me, that child.

I heard the stairs squeak. Dad was going to make the morning cuppa. I switched on the bedside table lamp, put my legs over the side and my feet into the slippers on the mat. Hopefully, someone would have bought some fluffy slippers for Christmas; if not, I would go to the Sales as I was in need of some which had some substance and warmth instead of the elderly fur-free pair that met my feet on that Christmas Day morning.

I went to the bathroom and then down the cushioned stairs. My parents had upgraded a lot in the house over the past three or four years ' ready for their retirement' when she hoped Dad would turn all of his attention away from the pharmacy and towards her.

"Morning Dad," I said, slipping my arms around him.

"Morning Love. Happy Christmas! Did you sleep well?"

"Like a log, thank you. Happy Christmas Daddy."

"I've made a pot of tea. if you could put the milk in a jug, we'll take a tray up to your mother."

It was quite like the old days although such family occasions always made me think of Stuart and I am certain that my parents felt his loss strongly at these times although they rarely commented.

Mum was eager to plan the day. Breakfast, our presents to each other, vegetables prepared for cooking, table laying and general preparation for the onslaught of my sister and her family. Mum was soon at her ablutions so I went into my room and made the bed. I wondered if there would be many more occasions when I would sleep in this room? Once Simon and I were married perhaps we would have George's old room which had been redecorated for use as the guest room? Thinking of this I shouted, " Where are you putting Simon when he arrives?"

"Oh. He'll be in the small room-if that's O.K.," added my flustered mother.

"Of course. I've no doubt you've sorted it out and got it ready for his visit," I replied.

"Hurry up you two. The rest of the family will be here before we've had breakfast if you spend all your time chatting instead of getting dressed," called Dad from downstairs.

"Always exaggerating," teased Mum, but I could hear her starting to rush around opening and closing drawers.

I chose to wear the dress that I'd had new last Christmas. It was scarlet and had a lovely black belt with it. As I pinned a diamante broach on to it I though that it was rather fetching!

Mum always cooked a ham at Christmas time which we ate for breakfast with home-made chutney and fresh rolls. Her idea was that after a turkey lunch, tea would consist of ham with pickles before scones with jam and cream and finished off with Christmas cake.

We then prepared the vegetables and everything was cooking when my sister and her brood arrived. We had opened our presents from each other and Mum and Dad had bought me the new slippers (a result of my hinting, although Mum would only have had to see the dilapidated state of my footwear on my last visit to know that I was desperate). They also gave me a new sweater in my favourite green, leather gloves and some cash for wellies! My siblings and their families had decided on Habitat tokens for household purchases although my nephews and niece had brought me toiletries as more personal gifts. We all had a lovely Christmas Day together, a quieter Boxing Day and then the 27th was upon us!

I hardly slept on boxing day night. Simon had promised a mid morning arrival and it was with relief that I answered his phone call at 10.35 to hear that the train had arrived safely and he would be glad of a lift; or should he get a taxi. My father and I got into the Humber and 'flew' to the station to pick up my 'nearly fiance.'

Once we were home Mum brewed coffee and we went into the sitting room; that same room where I had spent hours with Lizzie and the rest of my beloved family.

"Well Judith," began Simon, "I think I ought to give you your Christmas present." He gave me a huge parcel. I picked up a small package close at hand which I had lovingly wrapped and gave it to him.

"You open your box first," I said with a smile. He duly drew out the watch that I had purchased from Kemps. He smiled, put it on and lent over and kissed me.

When I had torn off the paper I reached my presents with a laugh. Simon had used a box he had found in the vestry which had obviously contained the communion chalice which the vicar had replaced in the summer.

"It was the only suitable box I could find," he explained.

"You could have pulled off the liturgical stickers," laughed Dad.

"I hope Matthew wasn't keeping the box in case the chalice needed returning," I said anxiously.

"We can preserve it and when I put it back in the vestry it will be as pristine as when I chose it."

136

At the bottom of the box, nestled in the corner, was the small precious container, which, when Simon lifted the lid, revealed the ring in its velvet hiding place. He took it and placed this precious symbol of our intentions on the third finger of my left hand.

"My Love," he said kissing me.

"Oh how lovely dear," cooed my mother almost overcome.

"My Darling," said Dad and he kissed me on the cheek and then turned to Simon and shook his hand. " Delighted," he enthused.

"How wonderful. We must let Lizzie know at once. Perhaps she can come over too. George, Belinda and the boys will be here soon for lunch and I'm sure we can make it go round. It's wonderful, Judith. Wonderful!"

Whilst Mum went to phone Lizzie, Dad went into the kitchen and opened a bottle of champagne to celebrate. Simon put his arms around me and drew me close.

"So, my Pickle. At least one set of parents are pleased. Let's hope my lot are as enthusiastic."

"Oh Simon. This is such a happy time. Thank you for making it so. I love you so much."

"Me too."

His lips met mine and I was utterly convinced that he was the man for me, for life.

When George and Belinda arrived with the family, Dad greeted them with, "Belated Happy Christmas." He picked up Michael, Mum hugged her eldest child and his wife and then picked up Stephen. My brother hugged me affectionately and Belinda did the same. George shook Simon's hand and Bee gave him a more perfunctory hug.

"We have something else to celebrate," beamed Mother who was never able to stop bubbling at exciting times.

"Yes," added Dad. " Come on boys I need your help."

Mum put Stephen on the ground and all the males followed Dad's command. She grabbed my left hand and displayed my lovely ring to Belinda who yelped with joy. By the time Dad and his entourage returned, everyone knew about 'Little Judith's' engagement as my brother teased.

"I hope you know what you're letting yourself in for," he said, turning to Simon who had heard all the childhood tales.

Simon replied, " Oh I've been well warned about her big brother."

"Right," replied George, "but I've changed haven't I, Bee? I really resented Judith joining our family once although she was only a few weeks old. We weren't really prepared for her; you know-no growing tummy on Mum or 'off' days, and when she arrived, M and D cooed over her and Lizzie grew maternal. I know I was rotten to her then but I hope I've made up since. Haven't I, Jude?"

"Of course you have Silly. Belinda has been a really good influence on you. Now you've got the boys you're nearly a normal person," I teased. Everyone laughed and Dad distributed glasses of bubbly for the adults and juice for the boys.

"To our lovely daughter and our nearly son-in-law. May you have happy days ahead."

"Thank you, Sir," smiled Simon. "I hope I make Judith as happy in her later years as you did in her early ones."

"That's such a sweet thing to say but she brought us so much happiness too," replied my mother.

"Does Lizzie know?" asked Belinda.

"Yes. I phoned her and they'll be arriving any minute."

"Great!" added George.

"We thought that an occasion like this needed the whole family," added Dad.

"I'm only doing a buffet today so I hope nobody minds," stated Mum looking around at us all.

"Of course not," replied Belinda. "I think we've all had enough of turkey and trimmings."

The ring was greatly admired, Christmas carols drifted in from the kitchen radio and the boys began playing with one of the games that Father Christmas had brought them. Cola began to bark and the back door opened to herald Lizzie's arrival. She almost ran to me, encircled me in her arms and said, "I'm delighted Darling."

We hugged and then it was Simon's turn.

"It's such lovely news. We both hope that you'll be really happy."

My niece Emma clutched my legs.

"Aunty Jude, Aunty Jude," she intoned.

"Hello Darling." I squatted down to Emma and James' height and gave them a peck on the cheek before rising to greet Thomas.

"Well done old thing," he said hugging me and then turning to shake Simon by the hand.

"Good to meet you. Thought you'd be a good chap from everything we were hearing."

Men are so odd especially those who have been to private schools like Thomas. I suspected that my birth father had been through a similar experience from what Libby had confided in me and I knew that my lovely father had attended a very minor public school before he went to university. They were all very good at knowing what to say!

More champagne arrived with some dainty hors d'oeuvres that mum had made. Simon and I were not big drinkers and only needed a small 'top-up.' Dad was enjoying playing host and Mum wore a permanent smile. The day was a triumph for all and I eventually made my way to my bedroom at 11 o'clock, anticipating a more trying day tomorrow at Simon's parents, but with happiness seeping through me as Simon kissed me good night.

In the morning we met at the breakfast table and Simon assured me that he had slept well in spite of the excitement. He'd probably had a better night than the one which I had spent and I suspect that as he had worked very hard in December he was probably very tired. He was also going back home to familiar people and it was my turn to be apprehensive about my reception. After all, Mr and Mrs Hutchinson were completely unaware of my impending arrival, not least as their future daughter-in-law!

We piled our presents and suitcases into my car and said our farewells to my parents and Cola.

"Don't be too long before you're home again. And think about a marriage date. There will be masses of preparation to do and I shall need to get invitations out," urged my dear mother. I gave her a hug and moved across to my father while Simon spoke to his future mother-in-law.

"We are truly blessed to have had you my lovely girl and now you have brought home a wonderful young man to be a part of our family. You'll make a fine partnership and one day a parish will welcome you to them. Meanwhile, live well and love long and may God bless you both."

"Thank you Daddy. Without you and Mum I'd never have reached this place at this time so we can all praise the Lord for what has happened. We must now 'venture forth' to Cirencester and meet my future in-laws. I expect they'll be fine, but may be a bit put out as they don't even know I'm coming."

"What?" asked my incredulous mother.

"Don't worry Mrs Harper. Mum's invited all the family today so one more can hardly matter and I sent them a Christmas hamper from Lewis's to ensure that nobody would starve."

"Well done my boy," beamed Father, patting his shoulder affectionately. "Anyway you must get going or it will be tea time before you arrive!"

Simon got into the passenger seat and we wound down the windows so that we could wave farewell. I turned the ignition key, felt the clutch bite in my trustworthy chariot and moved smoothly away from my four days of cosseting towards a potentially stressful situation.

CHAPTER 33

IN-LAWS,OUTLAWS

"Now don't worry Pickle. Remember, my parents have already accepted that their son chose to be a minister and their daughter married a plumber and electrician rather that a banker or accountant. They like Dave enormously now and adore the children. I even think they admire how Rachel brings up the kids and refuses to work until they are both at school"

I began to relax a bit and concentrate on the road while Simon recounted all that had been said both when we were together and when he was in all male company at the house. As we approached Cirencester, he directed me towards his home. Like most people he sounded proud of his home town as a child. His eyes shone as he pointed out his schools and the church which had led him into ministry.

"Raymond Taylor was a true man of God. He oozed spirituality, wisdom and faith. I always felt honoured that he had prepared me for my confirmation. In spite of his learned mind, he was able to connect with the questioning teenagers and started a youth club, which is why I am so keen on this area of ministry."

Once Simon got on to Raymond Taylor there was never any stopping him. As I knew he had lived in the parish I suggested that he came back to Earth and directed me to his parents' front door.

The house stood off the road and was approached down a curved drive. Although not as grand as my parents' house it would hold its own in a competition and was obviously lovingly maintained. As we drew up, a man (the double of Simon except for his white hair) and a woman, who was not dissimilar in appearance from my own mother, came down the steps to welcome their son.

"Darling. You've brought a lady-friend; how lovely." purred Mrs Hutchinson.

"Welcome home Simon," said his father.

"This is Judith," smiled Simon introducing me to his parents.

"Delighted," smiled Simon's father shaking my hand.

"How lovely!" added Mrs Hutchinson. "Come on in."

We went into a spacious hall which had three doors leading to other rooms and the stairs opposite the door rose towards the 'gods.' The door on the right stood open and we were ushered into a luxurious lounge. Obviously my future mother-in-law liked tasteful decor as all the colours toned together. Rachel and her family were already on their feet ready to welcome Simon and his 'lady friend.' After the formal introductions, Simon decided 'to take the bull by the horns' and announced,

"Judith and I have been seeing each other regularly during the year and I've asked her to be my wife. We became engaged yesterday."

"Oh! Why didn't you mention anything dear? You didn't even tell us when you phoned to say that you'd been delayed," said Simon's mother petulantly.

"Well....we weren't sure how things were going to turn out. The vicar wasn't well and I had to work an extra day so I wasn't sure when I'd be able to get away."

"So, have you already been to Judith's house?"

"Oh yes. That's where Father Christmas delivered the ring," smiled Simon, attempting to lighten the atmosphere.

"How lovely!" interjected Rachel who didn't want her mother's attitude to spoil such a special event in her brother's life. "I expect your parents were delighted?" she asked, turning to include me.

"Oh yes. They met Simon some time ago in Bristol. My brother hadn't had the honour but my sister has heard all the details about Simon from our long phone calls."

Seeing his wife's thunderous look Mr Hutchinson quickly asked, "So, did you meet at the church?"

"Indeed," smiled Simon drawing me protectively towards him. "We've been running a youth club there for the last few months, which is very successful."

"Well done you!" exclaimed Dave. "Teenagers aren't the easiest to manage."

"What do you know about teenagers?" asked the waspish woman who was to be my mother-in-law.

"That's what every generation says."

"Judith has no trouble with them. She teaches Religious Education at the school attached to the church and is very competent," asserted Simon.

"Well good, good," interjected Mr Hutchinson. " Are we ready for some pre-luncheon drinks? Perhaps you children will come and help Grandad."

Rachel stood up. "Shall I take orders?" she asked sweetly. "Mum?"

" A small sherry please dear."

"Judith?"

"Perhaps a sherry with a little tonic."

"It's not gin. Perhaps that's your usual tipple eh?"

"Oh no. I occasionally drink a little wine but I'm fine with sherry."

"That's a relief."

Was she usually this spiteful? Simon began to freeze next to me.

"May I have a sherry with tonic too? We've had it at friends' homes during the summer and it's more refreshing."

He got up and moved to sit by his mother. He took her hand and said lovingly, "Now Mother, look at this as gaining a daughter not as losing a son as they say."

"Oh I shall dear, don't worry about that."

She may not have worried but I was worrying seriously!

"So," she said turning towards me, "How old are your brother and sister?"

"George is the eldest, in his early forties and Lizzie's approaching forty. My younger brother Stuart died when he was just fifteen. A car accident. I'm the youngest."

"You're well spread out then?"

"Yes," I answered not wishing to go into details.

But Simon decided that his mother should know all the ins and outs.

"Beryl and Stanley Harper very kindly adopted Judith when she was only six weeks old."

"Oh. Adopted, eh?"

"Well yes," I replied. "They were really good to me and are the most wonderful people I have ever known."

"So, were you born to an unmarried mother or a foreigner, or a prostitute?" Her tone grew more horrified as she went through her list.

I decided to lie and told her that I had never traced my parentage. I was happy with the family I had and regarded myself as a Harper.

"Let's hope they think so too."

"Oh they do, Mother," assured Simon. "They are lovely people and certainly regard Judith as their own precious daughter."

Before any rejoinder could come from this 'mother-in-law from Hell,' her husband and his merry band of helpers arrived on the scene with the drinks. Once these had been consumed we were taken through to the dining room, which was across the hall from the lounge. Fortunately, I had been seated between Simon and Dave so I felt more at ease than when I was being interrogated by the matriarch of the household.

As it was the 28th of December, we were treated to a beautifully cooked joint of beef with Yorkshire puddings, roast vegetables, potatoes, peas and superb gravy. This was followed by a homemade apple pie with custard; all very delicious.

"Thank you," I said. " A feast indeed."

Mr Hutchinson decided he should propose the toast. "To my wonderful son, of whom I am immensely proud, and his delightful fiancee. May they be very happy in the years to come, and may God bless them."

We all drank as Rachel said, "Hear, Hear" and Dave tilted his glass toasting, "Here's to you."

My future mother-in-law drank slowly and never offered either a blessing or congratulatory word. I sensed that she and I would struggle to find much common ground. I hoped that Simon had inherited most of his genes from his father. He seemed to have a more generous disposition and certainly, Rachel was very pleasant. Perhaps I would be able to learn which tactics worked best with her mother from her? Or, was I going to have to spend my married life 'treading on eggshells'?

CHAPTER 34

BACK TO REALITY

I was so relieved to be home that day. Fortunately, once the lunch was finished it was only about an hour before Simon suggested that we should make tracks.

"Well, goodbye Judith," said my intended mother-in-law planting the French formal farewell on each of my cheeks.

"Thank you for your hospitality and the lovely meal. I hope that it wasn't too much of a shock for you. I'll try to be a good daughter-in-law and allow you a fair share of Simon," I said with a smile.

"I should think so, my dear. Remember who bore him and has known him longer than anyone," she chirped.

Now, how am I going to compete with that?!

Simon came to my aid, "Bye Mum. See you very soon." He put his arms around her and hugged her hard, "Remember I love you."

I told you that he knew what and when to say things. I decided that I would move slowly and carefully where mother-in-law was concerned. I stood back.

"Goodbye my boy," said Mr Hutchinson shaking his son's hand warmly. Putting his arm around me and kissing my cheek he continued, "And you, my best future daughter-in-law." These words made me feel wanted in my new family.

Rachel and Dave hugged and kissed us both, promising to join us for a weekend in Bristol before Easter, while their children danced around our legs before we were able to escape.

As we drove away Simon smilingly said, "Well that's all over. Now you're officially my fiancee and soon to be wife. We shall be far enough away for the family not to be a problem for you, so don't worry." Patting my knee he added, "You O.K. Darling?"

"Oh yes. I found your mother a trifle difficult, but expect it was rather a shock for her. You'd obviously not mentioned me at all in letters or phone calls, bless you."

"No. Poor old thing. But, you can see what she's like-'possessive', with a nasty tongue when the mood's on her. Mind, she can be the life and soul when she's the hostess and in charge. I guess we've all got used to her and don't take much notice of her various 'hats.' When someone new comes into the family she can be dreadful but we love her lots and I hope you will learn to love her too."

"Can't say I liked her attitude towards adoption. I think, in future, we shouldn't tell people I've been adopted. People can have a funny attitude, as your mother's reaction proved. After all I was only six weeks old. She was very judgmental. Doesn't she believe in 'judge not as ye be not judged' or 'let him who is without sin throw the first stone'?" I asked somewhat indignantly.

"Now, my love, let's not get bogged down with mother's opinions and beliefs. Suffice it to say that they attend church every Sunday and are kind and generous, up to a point. Although they were rather taken aback when I told them I had a calling to the church they went along with it and were delighted when I became curate at Saint Mary Redcliffe. When we get our own parish, Mother will be the first to brag about her son, the vicar," he said laughingly.

"It must have been awful for Dave when Rachel first brought him home."

"Oh yes. Although Mother said little to him directly; just made snide comments to Rachel. Fortunately I was away at university during the early days of their romance, so I only heard snippets from Rach' when I saw her at home. The parents had come round by the time of the wedding and now Dave's part of the furniture, particularly now Mum has her grandson and Dad his granddaughter. And one day we'll provide some more grandchildren."

"We'll have made it then!" I smiled, relaxing into the space that Simon's presence and voice made peaceful.

"Indeed! But you must have been pleased with yesterday. I was welcomed so warmly into your family."

"Yes. Mum has a great gift for making life better in her presence. I don't think it was always like that. Lizzie once told me that the older children had to learn to 'tread on eggshells' when she was in a mood. I can't say that I was ever aware of it, but I know she became gentler towards everybody after Stuart died."

"I know that was a terrible blow for everyone."

"It was. It changed George so much too. He was such a bully once. A shame it took the death of his little brother to help him grow up and show some consideration for others."

"What about Lizzie? How did she cope?"

"She was wonderful, just as you would imagine. She mothered me while Mum grieved and Dad was less than communicative with us all. She blamed George at first but she has a huge capacity to forgive and gradually accepted his love and friendship again once he came out of hospital. She loved Stuart very much so it must have been a bitter blow for her. She, like Mum, refused to let his memory go and often talked fondly of the things which he said and did. It took Dad a lot longer to grieve but we all came through the trauma and now here we are."

"Yes. Aren't we lucky?"

The conversation moved away from the last two days and Simon chatted about the services he had taken. Apparently the vicar's heavy cold stayed confined to his family. The congregation on Boxing Day morning was very small, but he had taken communion to a few people too infirm to make church which they had appreciated. Joyce and James Goodman had given him lunch and then he'd gone to Alice and Michael Jennings for tea. They had recently become parents to a baby boy so the house was littered with 'new arrival' cards, baby presents and Christmas cards and presents. Simon described it as 'a haven of haves and harmony.'

"I hope our house will be like that one day. They are rejoicing in little Jonah and each other."

"Hold on. We've got to get married yet."

"Yes and I've been thinking about that. Have you any idea when you'd like to become Mrs Hutchinson?"

"Well, if we married in the summer holidays I would go back to school as Mrs Hutchinson and if you haven't been offered a new parish, it wouldn't matter as you can move into my flat."

"That might work. I could suggest to the Vicar that I could keep my vicarage room as a work room; a study- cum- interview room. What do you think?"

"Sounds a good idea if he'll wear it."

"I'm sure he will. The vicarage is a huge house and I think he'll be glad to have the room used."

"I don't remember him being keen on us having the Youth Club meetings there though," I laughed.

"No. But interviews, etc won't entail too many teenagers and should suit everybody."

"You've convinced me, my love. So now all you have to do is convince the vicar. Do you think he'll be pleased to hear we are engaged?"

"I'm sure he will and so will everybody at church."

"Everyone adores you so they should all want your happiness."

"Bound to get a few spiteful remarks from the usual suspects so don't take any notice, will you? Just be your usual wonderful self and we'll surmount any problems with God's help."

"I know that but I'll be sad if people can't rejoice in our happiness."

"It's the way of the world, my Pickle. You'll have to toughen up to survive as a vicar's wife; we'll meet lots of difficulties."

"I expect I'll be able to carry on teaching?"

"Of course, Darling. Libby's bound to be supportive!"

"She thinks the world of you and is very pleased that we are a couple. I was dying to tell her that we were getting engaged but knew that we had to tell our families first."

I still hadn't told Simon that she was my birth mother. I did not want my friendship with her to be compromised in any way. I had already decided that she would come to the wedding as my best friend and then we would see how things developed. My parents would probably recognise her from the New Year photographs as I had done. One thing, for sure, was that Mr.& Mrs Malvern (if she was still struggling on) would not be invited. I would not want my birth mother's parents invading any more of my life. Was that wrong? What would our Lord have said? But it might make it awkward for Libby too. I felt certain that I had made the right decision. When we got home, we would have to start making plans for the 'big day' in July. Until then, I brought myself back to earth and concentrated on driving the few miles left before reality kicked in. Fortunately, we both had a few days before we were back into work, so we fully intended to continue in enjoying our new found commitment to each other.

CHAPTER 35

OUT WITH THE OLD...

On the 29th December Simon and I attended the early morning service so that we could speak to the vicar. He offered July 18th for our marriage, put it in the church diary, and told us that it would take precedence over everything else. He invited us back to the vicarage for coffee so that we could share our good news with his wife.

"I always knew you were made for each other," she smiled, hugging us both. "I know. How about we have a New Year's party so that we can all celebrate together?" she asked expecting an affirmative answer. "You, darling, can announce it as an open house and put up a poster on the notice-board. Yes?"

"If that's alright with Simon and Judith."

"Oh yes, that would be lovely," I answered.

Simon smiled.

"O.K. that's settled," he agreed.

"All hands to the pump then," Matthew said. "Simon, you type up the poster for the board and I'll make a note to include it in my own notices."

"I can decorate the poster if you like," I offered.

"Yes please, but don't say anything about the engagement. We can announce that at the party," said Barbara excitedly.

"You old romantic," teased her husband.

"Oh yes. Romance is still alive here," laughed my fiance.

"Meanwhile, I'll make us some coffee and get out some biscuits. You can come through when you've completed your tasks and have your earthly reward round the kitchen table," suggested Barbara.

It wasn't long before we were enjoying fellowship around her table, but then the phone rang and Matthew had to leave to visit a sick parishioner.

"It's a good job he's feeling better," said Simon.

"Fortunately, it's been mild for the time of year which has helped him recover quicker. At least he enjoyed his Christmas dinner on the day after Boxing Day. Christmas Day lunch was a bit of a wash-out, but we didn't have anyone important staying this year and the children were more interested in presents than food."

Almost on cue Ruth and Thomas appeared in the kitchen.

"Hello you two," said Simon.

"Thank you for our presents," replied the elder child Ruth.

"It's my pleasure," he assured them. "You have been lovely house mates and have always let me play with your toys!"

My heart warmed to his words. What a man!

"Would you like a drink of milk now?" asked their mother.

" And a biscuit?" suggested Thomas.

"If you promise to eat your meal later."

"Oh we will," assured Ruth, who remembered the day that she had been deprived of ice-cream after she refused to eat her main meal. Her mother was fair but always kept her word; whether a threat or a promise.

"That's a pretty ring," observed Ruth admiring the new adornment on my finger.

"Yes. Simon gave it me for Christmas."

"What did you give him?" she asked unabashed.

"This lovely watch," said Simon, pulling up his sleeve.

"Super!" said Thomas to everybody's amusement.

"Yes, isn't it? Everyone will be wanting one before you can say Jack Robinson."

"Who's he?" asked Thomas.

"Does he live in our parish?" added Ruth.

"No, it's just a saying. Simon could have said, 'before you can say wash your hands or tidy your room.'"

"Oh Mummy. You're always saying that."

"Well there you are. I'll have to say, 'before you can say Jack Robinson from now on'."

We all laughed. It was such a happy few hours. One day we would have a vicarage and children to brighten our days with their fun.

On the morning of the 31st December I answered the door to Simon looking worried. He had received a letter from his mother. As I read it I became furious.

"How dare she say these awful things?" I spluttered.

"We'll have to find a way to combat this before it takes control of her world."

She had implied that my roots could be less than equal to her family's, the children could be of mixed race, that my mother could have been a criminal, a liar or a woman of the streets. Nobody could be sure what was swimming in my gene pool and she would be 'DEVASTATED' to have grandchildren who would suffer from any of these eventualities.

"What can we do?" implored Simon.

"Well, you can write straight back and tell her that my parents were both university students with excellent brains. You can add, 'even if they had been brain dead and of a different race it would make no difference to the fact that we are in love and intend to marry'. Then ask her if she and your father can spare a few hours on July 18th to attend our wedding at Saint Mary Redcliffe, Bristol."

"That won't go down well," commented Simon.

"No, but it'll make sure that she knows you're a grown man who makes his own decisions now. Anyway your dad will make her see sense."

" You're right. Shall we write it together here and now?"

"O.K. my love. Let's get it over."

I had phoned my parents the previous evening to tell them that we had arranged with the vicar to be married on July 18th. Mum was initially disappointed that the ceremony would not be in her village church. After I had explained about Simon's position at Saint Mary Redcliffe and she had remembered the beauty of the church, she was soon won round. Dad, of course, was more pragmatic and told me to draw up a list of people to invite so that he and Mum could think about cost and choose a hotel to stay in.

Why do parents have to blight occasions over which they have no control? I presume that they have to change their role when the formative years are over. Perhaps this is what ' cutting apron strings ' is all about when you grow up.

Once the letter was written, I was anxious to get it posted before Simon experienced a change of heart.

"It could spoil the start of 1978 for her," he said sorrowfully.

"She'll get over it," I replied pointedly. "She'll not want to miss her boy's wedding and Rachel will be furious when she finds out. After all, your mother's bound to share our letter with her and then she'll have to answer why she received it. Don't worry. It'll all come out in the wash."

It must be hard for boys who have a strong mother with which to contend. After all, there's nothing like the love one has for a mother but, love of a wife or husband requires a break with the parental bonds, so Simon's mother would find it better to come to terms with this at an early stage rather than experiencing later angst.

That afternoon, we discussed who we would invite to our wedding and made a list. We decided that my parents could put a ceiling on the number of guests who would get the opportunity to enjoy the reception as they had already offered to meet the bill which was then customary.

Simon asked, " Who will you have as bridesmaids?"

"I shall probably have Emma and your niece, Mary, who are about the same age and perhaps Michael, Stephen and Lizzie's James could be page boys. Can you think of a job for Jonathan so that he doesn't feel left out?"

"I'll work on it. I believe you can have ring boys who carry the wedding rings."

"Yes. He could be my ring boy and carry your wedding ring and the best man could take care of mine," I said enthusiastically. "Are you having James Goodman or Michael Jennings?"

"Actually, I thought I'd have Andrew Myers, my friend from university. He trained for the ministry with me and has a curacy in the east end of London. He's a bachelor. When I had his Christmas card I remembered how fond I was of him so I phoned him and told him of our engagement."

"Was he pleased?"

"Indeed he was. Sent congratulations and said he hoped to come over and meet you soon."

"I think our calendar's going to be very full! I phoned Libby and invited her to the open house tonight, so she will know before we go back to school."

"That'll be lovely for you both," smiled Simon.

That evening we made our way to the vicarage where Barbara had prepared for the celebrations.

As we walked into the gathering a huge cheer rang out. Matthew had primed everyone and they had been invited half an hour before 'the honoured guests' who were announced when we came through the door. The thing about vicarages is that they have enormous kitchens which lend themselves to entertainment. Nearly everyone who knew us from church was in the room and Libby was standing next to Barbara. As I approached them the former put her arms out and hugged me hard.

"Wonderful news. I'm sure that you and Simon will be blissfully happy."

"Thank you. I'm so pleased that you were able to make it."

"I can assure you that wild horses wouldn't keep me away," she answered with a huge smile.

Barbara had organised everyone to bring a dish for the feast and these had been arranged around a cake on the large rectangular kitchen table. Mary, our organist, had iced a fruit cake with the words:

CONGRATULATIONS

MAY GOD BLESS YOU IN 1978

AND ALWAYS

"I thought it covered the New Year wishes as well," she explained in her quiet manner.

"It's lovely. Thank you Mary," I said planting a kiss on her cheek. She smiled with delight. As I went around the friends who had gathered I reflected on the wonderful celebrations which we had enjoyed and this made the hiccough with Mrs Hutchinson rather less painful.

Simon was, naturally, greeted warmly by his congregation and I watched with interest as he and my birth mother conversed with ease. Perhaps I should confide in him now? I certainly didn't want Libby to know as it could spoil our valued friendship. I knew that she had never broken my confidence, because Mum would have had to speak about it. Anyway, my sister appreciated how important it was for me to be Judith Harper (soon-to-be-Hutchinson!) daughter of Stella and Stanley and sister of George and Lizzie. We had always shared our secrets and thoughts, so why would this be any different? Matthew's shouts stopped my day dreaming. " Come and eat. We can't see in the New Year on empty stomachs. Anyway, I don't want to go out on the highways and byways to distribute this food after midnight. Simon! Judith! Start the ball rolling and others will follow you." We tucked into sandwiches, cheese and pineapple on sticks, cakes, peanuts and crisps.

At 10 o'clock Barbara suggested it was time to cut the large fruit cake. Matthew made a short speech.

"As we go into 1978, may we ask for God's blessing on this special couple, our church and God's kingdom. Simon and Judith, we thank God that you've been sent to minister here and pray that he will watch over you always and bless your intended marriage."

With this, some answered in 'Amens' and Barbara passed a huge cake knife to Simon who made the first cut. It was then whisked away by Barbara and she and Mary cut it into small slabs for all the people present. Simon thanked everyone on behalf of us both and proposed a toast: "To Saint Mary Redcliffe and all her people. May 1978 be a fruitful and fulfilling year."

After the cake and drinks had been consumed our trusty ringers left the party for the belfry to prepare to ring in the New Year. It was a most happy occasion and when midnight arrived the church bells pealed out and we joined hands to sing lustily 'Auld Lang Syne' as is the custom.

But, sadness often follows delight in life's pattern. Libby didn't make the start of the spring term. On the evening before, her mother was rushed into hospital and she was forced to return home to be at her bedside. Stella Malvern did not survive her latest heart attack and Libby was absent until after her funeral.

CHAPTER 36

...AND IN WITH THE NEW

My parents organised the wedding invitations immediately to ensure that their friends would keep July 18th free. The invitation list proved to be a difficult exercise. My parents wanted to invite many friends including Bernard Malvern whom they thought would like to see his grand-daughter married. I absolutely refused this suggestion, reminding them that it was Stella who wanted to trace me, and anyway I didn't want him there. Mum, encouraged by Lizzie, did not pursue the matter. Lizzie, of course, knew that I would be inviting Libby and was sufficiently empathetic to be aware of the problems that it might cause if her father came too.

Dad suggested that we found a suitable venue for the wedding breakfast; whatever that might mean. I consulted Barbara and Libby independently and both told me that they had been to pleasant wedding receptions at the Grovenor Hotel which was between Temple Meads Station and Saint Mary Redcliffe.

Simon decided we should go on a 'recce' which could stretch to a celebratory meal if we could fund one. All was up to our expectations and so we chose the hotel, booked it and Dad paid a deposit before Barbara could say ' tidy your room'. We asked Lizzie and Thomas, George and Belinda and Rachel and Dave if their children would care to be our attendants. They agreed, but insisted on paying for the material for the clothes, although they left me to choose the colour and style.

"I'll make them up," smiled Lizzie, who could turn her hand to anything. "I expect Mum will lend me a helping hand where necessary."

For the bridesmaids, I chose a pale green material and the dress would have a simple scoop-neck and full skirt, in the hope that they would be useful party dresses afterwards. Emma always looked pretty in pale green, so I knew Lizzie would be pleased with the choice. Rachel and Lizzie liaised over the girls' dresses and Belinda and her sorted out the styles suitable for small boys. Little Jonathan, the ring bearer, could wear a plain green tee shirt with dark green trousers which could be easily bought. It was all very exciting!

Lizzie and Mum came to Bristol during the Easter holidays and helped with the choosing and purchase of the bridal gown; a simple empire line style in satin. I bought a pair of white satin shoes, although later wondered when I would ever wear them again. I decided against a long train, preferring a small shoulder length veil held in place by a tiara. I decided to carry a small bouquet of white and pink rosebuds. The bridesmaids would have flowers in their hair and carry matching posies. Corsages would be of roses, white for the gentlemen and pink for the ladies.

With this in mind, my mother chose a cream dress and jacket with matching pink accessories and my future mother-in-law chose a pink dress and jacket with white ones. Both ended up wearing outlandish pink hats, but fortunately they didn't clash. Lizzie bought a simple navy suit with a pink blouse. When Libby and I went shopping together she decided to buy a crisp white dress with a pink stripe running through it. She chose a pink handbag, a pink and white hat and white shoes.

I came to terms with my own life. The more I got to know my birth mother, the more I understood why she had surrendered me and thrown away every opportunity to meet with me as her child. I now knew her well enough to know why she'd never wanted to be traced. She had experienced problems falling in love and had found the prospect of belonging to someone suffocating. Her ambitions did not allow her to take on motherhood or running a home for a husband and brood of children. I eventually decided that I would hold my own counsel and not tell Simon about our true relationship until after the wedding. I didn't want our special day marred by any embarrassing moments.

As the end of the summer term in 1978 loomed I prayed that I would emulate my adopted mother, because making a home and having a family lay ahead in my mind. I also prayed that the hen house Simon and I hoped to build would be a happy one and any eggs that we might hatch would be loving and giving to all.

Eventually my husband would be told the true facts so that I need not 'tread on eggshells' for ever.